Lady Ec

A
Published by Audrey Harrison

© Copyright 2020 Audrey Harrison

Audrey Harrison asserts the moral right to be identified as the author of this work.
This novel is entirely a work of fiction. The names, characters and incidents portrayed in it are the work of the author's imagination. Any resemblance to actual persons, living or dead, events or localities is entirely coincidental.
This eBook is licensed for your personal enjoyment only. This eBook may not be re-sold, reproduced in any format or given away to other people without the consent of the author.
Thank you for respecting the hard work of this author.
Find more about the author and contact details at the end of this book and the chance to obtain a free copy of The Unwilling Earl.

Chapter 1

London 1816

Ralph Swanson, Earl of Pensby, Viscount of Lymm, walked through the open door of the large Palladian building into the dark, chilly evening. The door was closed behind him by one of the ever-attentive footmen who were always on duty to pander to the patrons, whilst also keeping the peace in the barely civilised gaming hell Ralph had just left.

He dug his hands deep into his pockets and hunched his shoulders as he walked into the night. His expensive tailor would have repined at the rough treatment of a frock coat made of the finest material and sculptured to hug to perfection a well-defined body, but its wearer had no compunction about abusing his clothing in such a way.

He wasn't even concerned that he could be considered foolish, a fully paid up member of the *ton*, walking alone through the streets of London in the dead of night, oblivious to what was going on around him. Everything about him screamed wealth, a clear sign to those looking for an easy target to rob, but such issues were not considered by Ralph as he trod steadily through the darkness. He was beyond caring about such trifling matters.

Anyone watching his progress, taking note of his dejected gait and the way his body was almost folded in against itself would probably consider him a poor subject to rob in any case; his clothing might look fine but he had every characteristic of having lost a great deal within the walls of the establishment he'd made his exit from.

Before he turned the corner, the door of the gaming hell he'd just vacated was opened once more and a second gentleman hurried down the steps, turning in the direction of Ralph's hunched figure.

Ralph didn't falter upon hearing the footsteps behind him, just carried on towards his own accommodation, putting one step before the other, his eyes not really focusing on what he was seeing.

The second man, on catching up to Ralph, smiled at him as he fell into step alongside. "Thought you were going to make Eddie cry in there," he said amiably.

"He shouldn't gamble what he can't afford," came the shrugged reply.

"Half the gambling houses would close overnight if everyone adhered to that train of thought."

"I'll send his vouchers around to him tomorrow, hopefully he'll learn from his lesson."

The second gentleman looked at his friend in surprise. "You wouldn't expect him to do the same if your roles were reversed."

"No."

"Then why the deuce would you do such a deed for him? He knows your reputation at the gaming tables. Everyone does. Even I'd heard of it in France!"

A slight sneer flittered across the passively bored features. "Now you are coming it too brown, Longdon. Or trying to."

Miles Stanley, Earl of Longdon, smiled at his friend. "How the devil did you think I knew where to find you when I returned to England? I'd been out of the social whirl for so long, barely anyone remembers me. I needed to seek out old friends before I could be accepted back into the fold."

"Hardly. You and your fellow men are the returning heroes. Putting your time to good use, fighting for king and country, whilst I honed my skill on the gaming tables. You must despise men like me," Ralph said with a flicker of a glance in his friend's direction.

"Not at all," Miles said easily, walking alongside the hunched form, his own gait, the tall and straight stance of a military man. "I'm glad most people didn't have to see some of the sights I witnessed. You were the first born and had responsibilities at home, I wasn't. There are few first-born heirs on the battlefield. They are too precious to lose."

Ralph looked at his friend. "Your family has had a cursed rough time of it."

Miles supressed the sigh. "Yes, I never for a moment expected to inherit the title. Mama and my sister bore the brunt of what happened. I was abroad, firstly in America and then France and I admit reluctant to return when I heard Pa had died. He would have understood why I wished to stay with my unit. But then to have three members of the family die in total, one after the other, was cursed rum luck. I didn't expect my two brothers to follow Father to the grave so quickly. Edith suffered the most though. Mama isn't made of firm stuff for even the best of times. I feel she was difficult to deal with, but Edith never mentioned it in all of her letters. She's the real trooper of our family, not I."

"And you are now repaying her by escorting her all about town."

"Yes. Although I would enjoy it more if my long-time friend accompanied me sometimes," Miles said with a pointed look.

Ralph laughed. "Not me. Gaming hells aren't necessarily satisfying, but at least they aren't as tedious as the routs and balls that fill up the season."

"I hope one of those events will provide a decent husband for Edith. She's past her prime though. Poor girl spent three years in mourning and then was further delayed by Mama's refusal to visit London without my accompanying them. She'll be lucky to find a suitable suitor. You know how everyone clamours after the newest debutantes, the older girls are too often disregarded."

Ralph cast a sideways look of amusement at his friend. "She's an heiress and cannot be more than two and twenty, surely? I doubt she would appreciate your bleak outlook about her future."

Miles grinned, unrepentant. "As your paths have rarely crossed, I'm safe in voicing my concerns to you. Anyway, she's actually three and twenty and believes in a love match, so you see how poor her situation actually is."

Ralph shook his head at the brother's apparent callous dismissal of his sister's future but refrained from saying anything. He knew Miles to be a decent man who would do what was right by what remained of his family. Ralph could learn a lesson or two from his friend if he had the inclination to. He was trying to do the right thing in his own way but wasn't convinced he was achieving his aim.

They halted at Miles' house on Curzon Street. "Would you like to share a glass or two of port?" the slightly younger man asked.

"No. Thank you. I've the urge to leave London for a while and want to get a good start tomorrow," Ralph responded.

"Oh? Leaving for sport?" Miles asked.

"No. I have business on my estate," Ralph explained. It was a partial falsehood, but was a reasonable lie to prevent any further questioning by his friend.

"Oh. That's a pity. I was hoping to persuade you to come to a dinner Mama is holding next week. It'll be a dreary thing, so I need all the company I can muster," Miles said.

"As tempting as your invitation sounds, I'm afraid I shall have to decline. I shan't be returning to London immediately," Ralph explained.

"I've yet to see you at any ball, rout, or concert. You seem to be hiding from society," Miles pointed out.

"It's better that way," Ralph shrugged.

"I, at least, would enjoy your company if you did venture out more."

"Thank you, but I don't wish to provide fodder for the nosey beaks who also frequent the delights you mention," Ralph said. It wasn't exactly true, but it was a convenient excuse.

"It's not as bad as that."

"Is it not? They wouldn't whisper behind their fans at the appearance of the renowned gambler? I'd prefer avoid most of the cliques and groups which exist, which I'm sure is a mutual feeling."

Miles suppressed a sigh. "I thought you might be more persuadable after a night of heavy drinking."

"I'm never too bosky to make a mistake like that," Ralph said with a modicum of amusement.

"It was worth a try."

"I might join you on one or two occasions when I return, but only one or two," Ralph conceded taking pity on his friend.

"Excellent! I knew you wouldn't let me down!"

The friends shook hands, wishing each other well, before Ralph turned to continue on his solitary journey, hunching his shoulders once more, his head lowered as he walked. His boots echoed on the empty pavements, which within a few hours would be filled with the hustle and bustle of a busy London season.

Feeling slight amusement at Miles' attempt to include him in his family's entertainments, his face darkened; what he had to face at home prevented him being at the forefront of society, even if he'd wanted that for himself. He wasn't sure for how long the reality of his homelife could remain a closely guarded secret, but he was going to try and keep it that way. The *ton* didn't look favourably on something which went against their sense of perfection and his history did exactly that. The people who attended the gaming hells he frequented didn't give a fig who you were, or how you came to be there. As long as you could pay your way and spend a lot, you were given a welcome. Miles had been there only because he sought out Ralph from time to time, he certainly didn't lead the dissipated lifestyle that many of the patrons did.

Stepping onto the stone step which brought him to his own house, he opened the door with his key. Having instructed his staff not to wait up for him, he entered the empty hallway. One candelabrum remained lit on a marble table in the entrance hall.

Casting aside his hat and gloves, he caught sight of his reflection in the large mirror positioned over the side table. Grimacing at his pale complexion and his hardened stare, he could see nothing of note in his sharp features, dark eyes and jet hair. He looked the very devil he often mimicked. His features meant he did not have to act very hard to maintain the image.

Pausing for a moment, he recognised the all too familiar expression in his eyes. Oh, he didn't let anyone else see it, but it was there every time he looked back at himself through a looking glass. It was pure desolation and loneliness.

Quietly voicing the words which always filled his consciousness, he whispered, "I shall not abandon her to that hell. I shall not. I can be a lone wolf. I have to be. I know what has to be done, but why does it sometimes seem so damned hard?"

Not waiting for an answer from his reflection, he turned and, picking up the candelabrum, he started his solitary climb to his chamber.

Another long lonely night loomed ahead.

Chapter 2

Lady Edith Stanley sat at the escritoire, dipping her ink pen into the glass bottle in the stand. She paused in the act of scraping the excess liquid off the nib and chewed the corner of her bottom lip, a habit she had when she was worried or unsure. She needed the right words but struggled to find them. It had seemed an easy task when first thinking of the scheme, but now, putting it into practice was a little more daunting.

Her thoughts were interrupted by the entrance into the room of her brother. She replaced her ink pen on its stand, unused, and slipped the still blank paper into the drawer before pulling closed the lid of the desk.

Moving from her seat to one near her sewing basket, she smiled at her brother. "I didn't expect to see you until after nuncheon," she said pleasantly.

"A pity mother doesn't expect the same," Miles responded ruefully. "She seems to think when she has risen early, we all should."

"Perhaps you were unwise telling her that you were used to rising with the lark when saving us from the dastardly Napoleon," Edith teased.

"When fighting the French it is necessary to keep one's wits about one. It isn't quite the same as being in London for the season. We both know how long into the night everything continues here. I need the mornings to recover, especially after the more dreary entertainments," Miles responded, flopping onto one of the more comfortable sofas in the room and stretching his legs out in front of him, lazily admiring the shine on his boots his valet achieved every day.

Edith smiled at her brother. "I shall order coffee for you."

"Already done, m'dear," Miles answered.

The brother and sister were very alike; neither could be described as beautiful, more likely to attract the compliment of handsome, or having pleasant features. Both had open expressions, and clear grey eyes. Their darker hair wasn't quite black enough to be interesting, but dark enough not to attract the condemning description of mousey brown. Each had an easy-going nature, which was just as well because of the trials they had faced.

Miles had returned from fighting with Wellington with all the outward signs of his old, jolly self, but those who knew him well noticed the slight frown which almost constantly marred his features, and the fine lines he now wore around his eyes and mouth. He rarely spoke of his time abroad and Edith was wise enough not to ask. She didn't want to remind him of a time in which he must have suffered; she was just glad to have him home. Many other families of their acquaintance had not been so fortunate.

"I hear I'm to escort you to the theatre tonight," her brother said with a barely suppressed groan.

"Yes, Mama wishes to be seen at the new production."

"You don't wish to go?"

"I expect I'll enjoy it," Edith shrugged, picking up her tatting and looking down at the intricate work.

"A whole, eagerly anticipated production damned by faint praise!" Miles laughed.

Edith smiled, glancing up at her brother. "I admit I've not settled into London life as Mama would like me to. I think overall, I'd prefer to be in the countryside. That makes me sound so rustic, does it not?"

"There's a hundredfold entertainments in comparison to what you've experienced these last few years. I thought you'd be pleased as punch, gadding about town."

"So did I. But I think everything is slightly marred by Mama's interrogation of me every time I speak to any gentleman I encounter. Even if I exchange a brief 'hello', I see her eyebrows raise in question and hope," Edith admitted gloomily.

"She just wants to see you well-situated. We both do," Miles soothed.

"I know, but don't you think—" Edith started before seeming to change her mind.

"What?"

"I'm Lady Edith Stanley, a nearly-on-the-shelf, heiress. The fops who have not stood a chance with the latest debutantes feel I will be grateful for their condescension and attentions if and when they are not otherwise engaged. They are sure of my accepting any one of their offers, should they make one. Some are quite open that they will only make the offers at the end of the season when they've tried every other spinster. It's quite insulting."

Miles laughed despite his sister's angry expression. "The fools! Do they really make it so obvious that that is their game?"

"Oh yes, most certainly," Edith responded through gritted teeth. "The smile might remain on my lips but I admit to stamping on a few toes during a dance, in the most innocent of ways, of course. Usually after having just rejoined a set in which my delightful partner, whoever it is at that particular time, has informed me that a woman at my time of life should be grateful for the attentions he is bestowing on me. *And*, to add to the benefit of his condescension in noticing me, that I can expect to become more popular with others of our acquaintance because of his regard."

Miles let out a crack of laughter. "What a bunch of feeble coxcombs we are surrounded by! I didn't realise it was as bad as that."

Edith smiled, amused, despite her feelings of anger when the incidents were actually taking place. "I wouldn't mind so much, if it wasn't repeated by so many. I must have one of the worst dancing reputations in London for the way I crunch down on their precious toes. One or two of them have turned rather peaky at the encounter. It is vastly satisfying."

"I expect it is," Miles responded. "Oh, my poor girl. Give me a hint whenever you are offered such an insult and I shall sort the bounder out."

"I will do no such thing!" Edith responded. "I'm not the heroine of some gothic novel, who needs rescuing by her older brother. I can put up with their stupidity for a half-hour dance. None of them will be receiving an acceptance should they be foolish enough to make me an offer. Especially when they've been refused by every other potential bride."

"If anyone asks to pay their addresses to you, I know to ask about your dancing encounters before giving them my approval."

Edith smiled, her eyes glittering with amusement. "Yes. It's your way of finding out who to refuse on my behalf. At the moment though, I can't see there being anyone who I would esteem enough to seriously consider as a husband."

Miles stopped smiling. "That's a shame, if that's the case."

"Why? You haven't found a wife yet and you are eight and twenty," Edith pointed out.

"In danger of sounding like one of the fools you are already encountering, it's different for you, m'dear," Miles responded apologetically.

Edith's eyes flashed, all amusement gone. "A woman with an independent fortune doesn't have to accept a proposal if she doesn't wish to. And she certainly shouldn't have a time limit on when she needs to be married by."

"No, but I can't see you becoming an eccentric about town, or being a hermit in the country, nor can I see you not wishing to have a handful of children of your own," Miles said.

All anger dissipated, Edith smiled. "Yes, you know me well enough to be sure I'd like to have a large brood."

"Well, that's settled then, we'll have to find a man who can come up to snuff!"

"Hmm," Edith responded, casting a guilty glance at the seat she'd vacated on her brother's entrance.

*

A week later and Edith was seated at the same escritoire, but this time scribbling with determination. She cast away sheets of paper as if they were fallen leaves, completely disregarding the expense of such wasteful actions. Her fingers were marked with ink, as were the sleeves on her cotton day dress. Her lip was well chewed and a frown was firmly in place as the task she was undertaking seemed to overwhelm her.

She had spent a trying morning being subjected to a tirade of recriminations from her mother. Lady Longdon had discovered that one of Edith's potential suitors had mentioned that he was going to speak to her brother and that Edith had told him in no uncertain terms that he should not waste his breath.

"But, Edith, he was eminently eligible," her mother wailed, sniffing her smelling salts in an all too familiar dramatic way. The layers of lace on her dressing gown seemed to shudder with every word she uttered, creating an effect of a wobbling blancmange, which did nothing to encourage gravity on Edith's part.

"If I was blind and deaf, perhaps," Edith conceded, longing to escape from her mother's bedchamber and knowing there would be no chance of her removal until the older woman had said her piece at least twice.

"How can you speak so? He was besotted by you. He spoke in the most fervent of accents, when he sought my support for his suit. He realises he should have sought Miles out in the first instance, but I assured him that as I have been the head of the family these last few years, my word carries some sway in the family," Lady Longdon said.

"I'm sure he was well versed in what to say. He's had plenty of practice this week, proposing to Miss King and Miss Grayson before it was my turn. The fool mustn't have thought I'd find out about his previous choices even though Susan King is my best friend," Edith pointed out, not unreasonably.

"He expressed most sincerely how he had made a mistake in those cases. Men are wont to change their mind, Edith. They aren't as steadfast as we are, it isn't in their nature," Lady Longdon said, trying to be patient and offer her daughter the benefit of her advice.

"I accept that a person can fall in love more than once in a lifetime. It would be a sad state of affairs if it wasn't the case. But in the same week? Three of us? Mama, it's coming it too brown, it really is if you expect me to believe he has any affection for me," Edith argued.

"Your phraseology is appalling for a young lady," Lady Longdon scolded. "Why can't you be a dutiful daughter and accept my counsel? I am far more experienced in these matters. I can give you guidance and I say Mr Chumley is a good match for you."

"The fact that you actually believe that is quite depressing," Edith admitted. "Mama, he'd never make me happy and I know without a shadow of a doubt he'd regret marrying me within a week at the most. I need someone who wants more than my fortune. *I'm* more than my inheritance."

"Don't be foolish, at your age you have little to recommend you other than the money you bring to a marriage," Lady Longdon scolded. "There are debutantes aplenty to turn any young man's head, and it equally applies to the older men for that matter. Everyone is looking for a young woman who can provide many children, a happy home and, for some men, look after him in his dotage. At your age you must see the hopelessness of your situation."

Edith was dumbfounded. "No. I don't actually."

"And that is why I shall always consider you a foolish chit. Please leave me be, Edith. I have the headache and you are the cause of it. I can't bear to see your disobedient face any longer. It pains me."

The chastised daughter thus stood and kissed her parent. "I'm sorry to cause you pain, but I can't marry just anyone, even to please you, Mama," Edith tried to explain.

"You shall remain a lonely old woman then," came the damning response.

Edith was stung by her mother's view of her and walked out of the chamber seeking refuge in the morning room. Placing her arm on the cool marble of the fireplace, she rested her head on top of her arm. She felt adrift. Her father would have understood, he was more like Miles' character and her own. He'd been more inclined to challenge what was considered normal and strive for the best he could achieve. How their parents had made a match of it through the years said more about the patience of her father than it did of her mother's character. Although, how they'd become to be married in the first place, Edith would always wonder at; they seemed so different.

Walking to the window, she looked out onto the busy street. Carriages and horses passed by, all intent on reaching their destinations, all engrossed in their own lives. People walked, some hurrying, some dawdling on their way. Not for the first time, she wondered about their lives, did they feel as lost as she sometimes did? Were they content with their place in the world? She wished she was.

It wasn't just London she was dissatisfied with. She loved the country and had always felt at home there. She could have coped with a season in London, if there hadn't been other emotions swirling through her and causing her to feel completely unsettled. Those were harder to shift in the city. Here she was away from everything which was familiar to her. Time and again she was reminded of her shortfalls;

she couldn't find a husband who she could both love and respect; she was a disappointment to her mother by remaining single; she couldn't bring the smile back to Miles' eyes no matter how much she tried; she missed her two brothers and father so desperately it physically hurt. It all added to her feelings of discontent and sadness.

She set her shoulders. She'd given the season enough opportunity to provide options for her future. It was time she took hold of her own destiny and found her own life partner, one who would be a likeminded companion, not a resented fop. There must be someone out there who would be a good match. After all, she didn't have to consider finding a man of fortune, which made the fact that she hadn't met anyone she thought highly of even more frustrating.

A short time later she was disturbed by her brother, but this time her activity was harder to hide.

Miles walked into the room and paused in surprise as he saw the spread of papers on the desk. "Have you spent your whole quarter's allowance on paper?" he asked.

Edith blushed, hurriedly trying to gather the papers together. "I'll replace what I've wasted."

"What is so difficult that has caused so much to be cast-off?" Miles asked, crossing to the desk in curiosity.

"Stop!" Edith said, raising her hand to stay her brother. "It is of a personal nature. Don't come any closer until I have cleared everything away."

Miles narrowed his eyes at his sister. "Have you embarked on some sort of clandestine correspondence?" he demanded.

Edith glared at her brother. "Don't be ridiculous!"

"In that case there is no need for secrecy."

"I'd like to keep some things private, if you don't mind."

"There isn't a chance of that when you're acting all havey-cavey," Miles said and with one deft movement he moved forward, grabbing one of the sheets of paper from the pile Edith had clutched in her hands, and strode over to the window to read it.

Edith let out a shriek of complaint, but trying to grasp the sheet with one hand, so she could still protect the others, was a fruitless task. Miles held firm, holding his sister at bay with one outstretched arm.

"*Eligible, independent Miss S, with lively mind, passable features and quick wit, seeks gentleman who can appreciate such qualities and enhance the said lady's time in London. Only single men need apply and for sincerity and security a correspondence will be required before any meeting occurs. All serious replies will be given due consideration. A good mind and kind nature are more important than good looks and fashionable dress*," Miles read out loud, his voice incredulous. There was a moment of quiet when he'd read the paper before he turned to Edith, his hand no longer preventing her approach. "What the deuce are you thinking, Edith?" he asked in disbelief.

Edith's face was aflame with embarrassment. She had known how it would be. Miles was about to voice the same thoughts which had kept her awake at night. That was until she had come to the decision that it was the only option she had to gain the sort of future she longed for. "How else am I to find a husband beyond the men I have already met?" she asked defensively, not quite meeting Miles' gaze.

"You are asking every blockheaded buffoon to respond to this! Any fool will think they have a chance with your words!" Miles exclaimed.

"No, they won't. I'm hoping it will appeal to man who is respectful and who I can respect in turn."

"*A good mind and kind nature are more important than good looks and fashionable dress,*" Miles quoted derisively. "That's every unmarried hunch-backed, squiffy-eyed, tongue-tied, fubsy-faced literate man within ten miles of London about to send you a missive to offer for you."

"Don't be ridiculous! Of course, that won't happen. Most men require a fortune, I haven't hinted at my having one," Edith snapped.

"You have stated you are independent. Only a woman with funds would use that term. You might as well have said 'available single heiress is desperate', for that's how it will be received," Miles said a trifle cruelly.

"I'm not desperate!" Edith snapped, stung at her brother's words.

"Surely… surely there is someone within our circle who would suit you? Perhaps you haven't been fully open to considering some of the men you've been introduced to?" Miles suggested gently.

"I'm not so high in the instep that I have been wandering around town thinking I'm too good for the men I meet, if that's what you are thinking."

"No. I wouldn't suppose that for a moment," Miles responded.

"And I'm not so shallow or foolish enough to aim for the nonpareils of the season! I might not consider myself quite as much a lost cause as mother does, but I'm also not deluded," Edith said tartly.

"Where were you going to advertise this?" Miles demanded.

"In *The Times* of course," Edith explained. "It's all done very discreetly. They compile all the answering letters and then send them on to me in one parcel. There is no danger anyone responding to my advertisement will find out who I am."

"This is madness," Miles said.

"It's a perfect way of finding someone I might not meet in a ballroom."

"So, someone outside your social sphere?"

"Not necessarily," Edith cajoled. "None of us meets everyone in our society and who knows, my striking warrior of a soldier brother could be off-putting for some men."

"Only a wet lettuce," Miles scoffed.

"Everyone reads the advertisements. You must have done so yourself."

"Only to ridicule the wording of the more outrageous ones," Miles said, picking up a copy of the newspaper Edith had been using to try and gain some inspiration. Miles started to read some of the comments in a false, high-pitched voice. "*Slim ankles and a pretty nose*," he mocked. "*I can sew well and play the harp. My drawing skills are exceptional. My wish to find a husband to cosset is my most wished for aim in life.*"

"Stop!" Edith gurgled with a laugh. "There are some serious descriptions in there. You're just choosing the more foolish ones to justify your derision."

"I'm trying to show you that your idea is foolhardy," Miles responded. "I know I tease you about your age and possibilities, but your situation isn't so wretched as to resort to something like this."

"I know that. This isn't an action borne out of wretchedness, I assure you."

"It's an act of folly."

"I'm trying to put my destiny and wishes into my own hands. I refuse to wait until I'm so disheartened that I accept one of the patronising buffoons I'm currently forced to be pleasant to," Edith said primly. "I'm sending this off."

"I hope you won't live to regret it," Miles cautioned. "But, you are of age and can make your own decisions. As long as it brings no shame onto the family name there is little I can do to stop you."

"I suppose that's almost a statement of support," Edith smiled.

"I wouldn't go that far," Miles said dryly.

"Please don't tell Mother," Edith begged.

"Good grief! Do you take me for a nodcock? Neither of our lives would be worth living if she found any of this out. Just promise me you won't put yourself into any situations in which you could be compromised. Without doubt there will be blaggards who respond."

"I shall be careful," Edith promised.

Miles didn't look convinced.

Chapter 3

"Good God, Edith, tell me you won't be replying to all of these?" Miles said, storming into the morning room where his sister sat. He marched over to her and roughly placed a large pile of letters next to her. "I told you it was folly!"

Edith blushed, looking in awe and wonderment at the number of letters cascading over the sofa she was seated on. "Are they all for me?"

"Of course, they're all for you!" Miles snapped. "God knows what the staff think!"

"Thankfully, I'm not obliged to consider the thoughts of the servants in making life decisions," Edith responded stiffly.

"Those same servants talk to other servants in neighbouring houses. Don't underestimate the detrimental impact gossip can have, my dear, or you shall be leaving London shamed and ridiculed," Miles warned.

Edith sighed. "I'm sorry. I know gossip can get out of hand, but I had presumed the letters would come wrapped as a parcel, not separately like this. There are quite a few."

"The understatement of the year," Miles responded. "Well, come on, open them." He sat on the nearest chair, resisting the temptation to open some of the letters himself.

"I-I should open them in private," Edith stammered.

"Oh no you don't," Miles said quickly. "I'm not convinced you won't tumble head first into a disaster. I'm not leaving you until I'm certain you won't rush into anything foolish."

Edith glared, highly insulted that she wasn't trusted by her brother, but opened the first letter anyway.

My dearest Miss S,

I immediately knew we were destined to be together as one, the moment I read your darling advertisement. I long to appreciate and worship you as you should be…

"Oh dear," Edith responded, passing Miles the letter. "He's unsuitable."

My dear Miss S,

I have much to offer you. I can give pleasure to your mind but especially to your body that you have only dreamed of. I long to hear you call out my name, your voice filled with passion…

"Oh, my goodness me!" Edith gasped, flinging the letter on the floor. "I won't be responding to *that* writer!"

Bending to pick the letter up, Miles started to read. Growling, he tore the letter up. "Damned cur! If I knew who he was, I'd draw his cork for his base language and insinuations."

Edith chose to remain silent, not wishing for more recriminations as she went through each letter. Her heart sank as the pile of people she was rejecting became larger than the decreasing number remaining.

After half an hour, she sat back. "I suppose two potential matches is better than nothing," she said, trying to sound positive.

"Barely," Miles said with derision. "What now?"

"I write back, using *The Times* as the intermediary and see what information I can gather and to see if we feel there is a connection between us," Edith explained. "I know you think it's a fool's errand, but it might work."

"The first part of that statement is correct. I want your assurance, Edith, that you will not arrange to meet anyone before you are sure of their credibility. Any number of lies could be uttered between the sheets of a letter."

"Any number of falsehoods can be uttered face to face. I think a person reveals more of themselves through the written word." Edith defended her actions.

"Don't be so sure. An innocent like you can be taken advantage of any number of ways."

"Make up your mind, brother. One moment I'm a green girl, the next an old maid!" Edith snapped tersely.

Miles smiled. "You can be both."

"Oh, be quiet," Edith huffed. "When I am happily settled, you'll see the error of your ways."

"When you are married, I shall feel nothing but relief."

*

Ralph folded his tall frame into one of the leather chairs in Boodle's. It wasn't the club for the men who considered themselves the height of fashion, more likely to welcome country squires, or those who enjoyed deep gaming than the men who frequented Brook's or White's; it was a club on the edges of society which suited Ralph. He'd been away for two long weeks and had been suffering a persistent headache as a result. He'd invited Miles to join him. Friends since they'd met at school, there was a bond between them which others would be puzzled at. The open, friendly officer of the cavalry and the unsociable, reclusive gambler weren't an obvious pairing, but the two held each other in high regard.

Lifting a glass of amber liquid to his lips, he let the spirit slide down his throat before speaking to his friend. "Was the soiree at your abode a success of the season?" he asked of the event he'd missed.

"Oh, that? Yes, it went well enough, I suppose," Miles responded absentmindedly.

"Damned with faint praise," Ralph said drily.

Miles smiled. "Damned family more like."

"I can empathise with that wholeheartedly. I thought your sister at least was a sensible being, not prone to causing you any concerns."

"She wasn't, until she came up with the most foolish, hare-brained idea a chit could ever utter," Miles said through gritted teeth.

Ralph's eyebrows rose. "Sounds interesting."

"Interesting is not a word I'd use. Oh, I shouldn't be speaking of it," Miles admitted. "If the story gets out, she'll be ruined."

"I hardly pass the time of day with the gossip of friends," Ralph pointed out.

"Only because I'm your only friend," Miles teased.

Ralph raised his eyebrows, taking another drink before speaking. "And the ladies in society consider you to be such a gentle-natured beau. If only they knew the truth. You have hidden claws my friend and they are sharp."

"Oh, don't take on so," Miles grinned. "You know I regard you as one of the best dashed fellows around."

"Someone has to, I suppose," Ralph drawled. "Now, what's this with your sister?"

Miles recounted Edith's scheme and didn't hold back in voicing his opinion of it. Sitting back after finishing the whispered tale, he ran his hands through his hair. "I can tell you, it has me having nightmares as to the hundred ways it could go wrong."

"Yes. She's taking a huge risk, but in some respects I admire her for it," Ralph admitted.

"Really?" Miles asked, astounded.

"Why yes, she's trying to take control of her own destiny. I can see the attraction of that," Ralph explained. "Too often one is affected by the situations around them and feels somewhat out of control."

"A damn fool way of going about it," Miles insisted

"Perhaps, but she's right in the fact her options are limited. You obviously haven't introduced her to the right calibre of beau since the season started," Ralph said.

"She's too fussy. I'm beginning to think my mother could be right in that she's not going to make a match of it at all," Miles admitted for the first time.

"And she wouldn't be allowed another season? It is only her first after all."

"Would there be any point? She'd be four and twenty by then; she'd likely spend most of her time on the wallflower benches. What's the point in making all the effort of spending the season in London for that?" Miles asked.

"Still an heiress though," Ralph pointed out.

"Hmm."

"You act as if she has three heads. Surely she is personable? I'm presuming she has your penchant to please? I know we have met, but it was some years ago, she wasn't out of the schoolroom, I seem to recall."

Miles grimaced. "She might be a little more caustic than I," he admitted.

Ralph laughed. "I suddenly have the overwhelming urge to meet this dragon of a sister."

"Good, you can join us at Vauxhall Gardens tomorrow night. There's a concert and firework display on. I've hired a box."

"I walked into that one, didn't I?" Ralph scowled.

Miles laughed. "You did but please don't let me down."

*

Ralph called at Curzon Street in his carriage to collect his friend and his relations. Entering into the hallway, he was greeted by Miles.

"Welcome! Mother and Edith shall be with us shortly. Would you like to join me in a glass of brandy in the library?" Miles offered.

"Thank you, no. I'm happy to wait here for them to join us, if they won't be long. There's no need for us to keep the ladies waiting," Ralph said.

"You really are looking forward to tonight, aren't you?" Miles grinned at Ralph. "Can't wait to get there, so you can leave as soon as it's acceptable that you make your escape. I hope I can come with you."

"Said by a dutiful son and brother," Ralph responded.

"Spend an evening with my family and you'll understand what I mean."

"How rude you are, Miles." Edith's voice came from above the two gentlemen. "You put my mother and I to the blush."

"As mother is not within earshot and you wouldn't be cruel enough to repeat my words, I'm only in danger of hearing your scolding, which is the lesser evil of a situation to be in," Miles responded with a grin to his sister.

"You are the most dastardly of brothers," Edith responded, walking down the stairs, her hand trailing along the bannister rail. She was dressed in a lilac silk gown, which suited her colouring perfectly and skimmed over her tall, slim frame. Not one for wearing the whites and creams of the debutante she was, she tended to wear pastel colours instead. She wore simple diamonds around her neck, an elegant droplet design, and crystals in her hair. A bracelet over her long silk gloves completed her ensemble and with only a touch of lip colouring, she looked regally handsome.

"Lady Edith, I tend to ignore your brother as much as I can," Ralph said smoothly, bowing over Edith's proffered hand. He had felt a moment of stillness when he'd first looked up and seen Edith. She seemed effortlessly graceful and unaffected, her sparkling eyes laughing at them both as she descended the stairs. He wanted to ask Miles what was wrong with his sister, for in looks and demeanour, he could find no fault. Why she was unmarried seemed preposterous if even his jaded eye could see her beauty. For to him she was beautiful.

"As I try and do the same, I cannot fault your reasoning," Edith said with a smile. She had noticed the intense look Ralph had given her and it had caused something to unfurl in her stomach. He was a striking man, all dark and angled features, who was exquisitely dressed. Miles always looked dressed to perfection, but his friend outshone him in Edith's eyes.

"Edith, meet Pensby, you already sound like you'll get on well," Miles said with a glower.

"With you offering insults to all and sundry, I expect it's inevitable," Edith said, accepting her shawl from a waiting footman.

Lady Longdon soon joined them, although the banter stopped once she joined the group. A woman inclined to moan and grumble, she soon drained the atmosphere of all its joviality.

Once they had entered their reserved space in Vauxhall Gardens, Lady Longdon was seated as comfortably as a woman with her tendency to find fault could be; Miles and Ralph took a more strategic position in the space, abandoning Edith to entertain her mother.

"I'll be glad when Mother returns to the country, I can tell you," Miles admitted, once out of earshot. "I know I'm an unfeeling brute, when I consider all she's lost, but she's not easy to be with. I feel heartily sorry for Edith sometimes."

"Yet, you've left her to her fate," Ralph pointed out, looking at the barely suppressed pained expression on Edith's face as she listened to her mother's chatter.

"I don't feel *that* sorry for her," Miles said with a laugh when he noticed Edith glaring at him, as she guessed some extent of what her brother was talking about.

Ralph smiled at the interaction. "You are fortunate you have a sister. Imagine if it was only you and your mother."

"Shudder at the thought," Miles grimaced. "Hopefully, some of her cronies will soon join her. I tell you, it's like a coven of witches sometimes in the drawing room at home. Terrifies me. A battalion of Napoleon's men didn't scare me as much."

Ralph gave Miles a mock arch look before approaching Edith. "Lady Edith, would you care to join me on a walk through the avenues before they become too crowded? Miles is happy to remain with your mother."

Edith sent a knowing look of laughter to her brother. "Why, yes, my lord, that would be perfect. Thank you."

"Take your shawl, Edith, the night is chilly," Lady Longdon said.

"Yes, Mama."

Edith and Ralph left the box and, accepting Ralph's offered arm, they started to stroll along the lit avenues, passing one or two other couples. The effect was to appear far away from the activities and offer people a little more sedate area. Very often these were used for illicit meetings, but so early in the evening they were enjoyed by those purely enjoying a stroll and the company they were with.

Edith was more than happy to be on the arm of such a handsome man. He was taller than her, like her brother, and although he hadn't experienced the exercise Miles had, he was still a broad-shouldered man. He had a face which didn't smile much, but Edith had seen him smile when talking to Miles and she had been fortunate he hadn't caught her staring. His features had changed, he'd looked younger and more carefree. Handsome features had turned into stunningly handsome.

"Have you known my brother long? I vaguely remember you visiting many years back, but as I was only allowed downstairs for the briefest of times, I can't recall much of those who visited," Edith asked.

"We've been friends since our first year at school," Ralph answered. "He took pity on me."

"I'm sure that wasn't the case, although he tends to like most people. He's very easy-going in that respect," Edith acknowledged.

"Yes. He is forgiving of the foibles of others. I'm glad he returned from Spain, America and France uninjured. A miracle to see so much fighting and return unscathed, not many others could claim the same, I'm sure."

"Relatively unscathed," Edith corrected. "I don't think anyone would survive the battles he did and be the same person as they went."

"True. He admires you for what you dealt with whilst he was away."

"It was hard," Edith admitted. "But my main aim was to shield Miles as much as possible. Mother wanted me to insist he returned but I refused. It might sound foolish, for he could have been wounded, or worse, but I know how much it meant to him to be fighting with his friends. If he'd have returned early and they had been killed…"

"Yes. His guilt would have been far worse than anything he suffers from now," Ralph agreed.

"Exactly! I know it could be seen as idiotish on my part, but I understood what was driving Miles and I couldn't interfere with that for my own selfish reasons. There was really nothing to be gained by him returning. Mother just couldn't see it," Edith explained, voicing her motivation for the first time. "In fact, no one I expressed my view to seemed to understand."

"Were they all ladies?" Ralph asked.

"Yes, I think so. Apart from the family solicitor, it was Mother's friends who visited us in the main."

"There you have it. They will have responded from the need to keep those they care about protected and close. If you'd said the same to the men of your acquaintance, I'm sure you'd have found understanding."

"That's an interesting point," Edith mused. "Thankfully he came back safe and Mama could finally be at ease."

"And he's taken over the family title. To his credit he seems to have been born to the role. Not that I'm saying he coveted it, for I know he didn't."

"He's shouldered the responsibilities without complaint. There have been too many changes over the last few years. It's been an emotive time for us all. I miss my father and my brothers. The house was always full of laughter and joviality when they were all together."

"It's hard to lose those who are close to us."

"Yes."

"Your brother enjoys teasing you," Ralph said, changing the subject onto a lighter topic.

"Far too much," Edith said with a slight smile. "He chooses his moments perfectly, usually when we are in company so I can't retaliate as I would wish. Instead, he knows I have to act demure and unaffected."

"He said you were a little more caus–fiery than he is," Ralph corrected himself quickly.

"I can just imagine what he actually said, yet he's a real fishwife when he starts," Edith countered, not being offended at the label her brother had given her.

Ralph laughed. "You don't idolise him as the elder brother to be obeyed and worship?"

"Oh, yes, completely, but there's no need to let him know that is there? Where's the fun in that?"

"True."

"Do you have siblings, my lord?"

"No. Unfortunately not. I have little family," Ralph answered, stiffening slightly.

Edith felt the movement under her hand, which had been until that moment, sitting comfortably on the firm arm and although she wondered at his answer, she didn't press further. "I'm glad I have Miles. Mother is sometimes difficult to manage."

"From what she has suffered in recent years, I expect she is justified in being a little out of sorts. It's important to appreciate and support our parents as best we can," Ralph countered.

"I am a dutiful daughter most of the time," Edith admitted.

"I do feel that doing our duty is the most important aspect of respecting our parents. In fact, I'd go as far as to say we owe it to them to be respectful."

"I try my best, but I can't always be what my mother wishes," Edith admitted.

"Is that because you rail against being told what to do?" Ralph asked, genuinely curious about Edith after what Miles had revealed to him.

"Do you always ask impertinent questions, my lord?"

"Only when I feel someone is perhaps a little misguided, or my curiosity is piqued."

"You seem very keen to go beyond the etiquette of polite conversation."

"If you want the boring conversation of the fops who surround you in society, I'm afraid you chose the wrong man to escort you, Lady Edith. I don't hold my tongue if I have something to say and I've been led to believe neither do you."

"That would suggest I'm an opinionated baggage," Edith responded.

Ralph laughed. "I've suggested nothing of the sort."

"If you were at this side of the argument you might view your words differently."

"Is that what we're doing? Arguing? I thought we were having a spirited conversation. I was obviously misinformed in your character. I was led to believe you were a little out of the ordinary. I beg pardon for being wrong."

Edith was discomfited and stung by Ralph's rebuke. She prided herself on being a little out of the common way, she was well aware of being proud of the fact. In the fewest of sentences, she'd been told she was no different to the hundreds of other young women in society. It rankled her vanity, something which she had convinced herself that she didn't have.

"And so, we enjoy a cose as we walk," Edith responded sarcastically. "I think it's time we returned to our box, my lord, before one of us is overwhelmed by the charm of the other."

"As you wish." Ralph set his lips in a grim line. He could have laughed at her comment; he had to give her credit for her rejoinder. It was no wonder she hadn't been a hit of the season. She pretended to be one thing, whilst being no different from the dozens of other vixens who prowled the ballrooms of society. This was exactly the reason he didn't socialise, one moment you were chatting amiably, the next some word or comment was misunderstood and you were faced with a missish termagant.

They returned to the box in silence. Miles raised his eyebrows at the serious expressions on both of their faces, but received no response from either Edith or Ralph. Edith was deposited with her mother once more, who was now surrounded by people she knew.

Ralph bowed to the group of ladies. "Please accept my good wishes, Lady Longdon, Lady Edith, ladies. I hope to see you some time soon." Nodding to Miles, Ralph left the box.

Miles looked slightly stunned as he approached Edith and motioned that she should leave the group gathered around their mother.

Edith reluctantly left the confines in which she couldn't be questioned, whilst in reality there was no point trying to delay speaking to Miles. "I said nothing," she said defensively before Miles had time to speak.

"That's an admission of guilt, if ever I heard one!" Miles exclaimed.

"He's quite opinionated and didn't appreciate when I didn't agree with his every word," Edith admitted.

"Oh, Edith," Miles groaned.

"What? All I did was stand up for myself when he became impertinent and offensive!" Edith said, flushing.

"Could you not, just for once, be nice?"

"I am nice."

"You are an acquired taste."

"Well! And you're supposed to be my defender!" Edith said with a huff. "Surely you don't want me to set my cap at Lord Pensby?"

"Ralph? Good grief, no. He ain't the marrying kind, but I'd like you two to get on. He doesn't mix in society much."

"There's obviously a reason for that!" came the tart response.

"Yes, there is. I don't know much about his homelife, but I suspect it's not a happy one. There is only himself and his mother. She's never seen in town, or Brighton, or anywhere as far as I can tell. Ralph clams up if one tries to find anything out about their situation, so I've given up trying, but it's clear that he's not happy and I was trying to bring him out a little more," Miles explained.

Edith looked mortified. "And I've put paid to that. Oh dear. I just thought he was criticising me because he was unpleasant."

"I doubt that very much. What motivation would he have, or what would he be hoping to achieve? I do wish you'd be more circumspect, Edith. That temper of yours will get you into trouble one of these days," Miles cautioned.

"Perhaps writing to perspective suitors is the safest way of securing a husband after all. Hopefully, whoever I chose will be smitten with me before he realises I have a quick temper," Edith said with a smile.

"Hmm. I hope you are being careful."

"I am, although one of the potential suitors didn't reply to the letter I sent in response to his. I can't understand why one would write to someone and then not continue with the correspondence," Edith said a little dejectedly. "Never mind, there are only a few more days and I should be getting my next parcel."

"Will it be a parcel this time?"

"Yes. I sent a letter to the editor, asking specifically for his discretion. I received a reply, promising me there will be no further mishaps," Edith assured him.

"I'll believe that when I see it," came the muttered response.

Chapter 4

Ralph pushed himself away from the table, emptying his glass as he stood. He smiled slightly. "Gentlemen, thank you for your company tonight."

"And our money," grumbled one of the still seated fellows.

"I didn't force you to join me," Ralph pointed out. "In fact, I'm quite happy to let you try and win it back."

"A fool, I might be, an idiot I am not," came the disparaging reply from one of his acquaintances who had been hit particularly hard by losses.

"I'll bid you goodnight then," Ralph nodded and left the group.

Leaving the building, he faltered before taking his usual route. Restlessness was affecting him these last few days and he couldn't settle at anything. Instead of turning home, he changed direction and headed for St James's Street.

Entering Brook's club, he was greeted with surprise, but welcome, by one or two of the gentlemen present.

"Have you decided to visit a higher class of gaming establishment?" Lord Hoylake asked, blowing a cloud of cigar smoke into the air as he spoke.

Ralph liked the man. There was no smoking allowed in the establishment, but Lord Hoylake didn't give a damn and flouted the rules. Most of the occupants preferred snuff than the newer cigars, which were seeping into the country since the men returning from the Peninsular War had brought them back with them.

"I don't know about that. A change of scenery seemed appealing," Ralph answered, ordering a drink from an attentive footman.

"Heard your luck was having a good run. I'd be willing to put it to the test," Lord Hoylake offered.

"Maybe another night. I'm bored of cards tonight."

"Bored of cards, by gad man! Are you ailing?"

Ralph smiled and accepted a glass of amber liquid from the servant at his elbow. "Perhaps. I doubt it will be of the long-lasting sort though, so you'll have that game."

"I should hope so. The profits of half the gaming hells in London would sink if you were to reform."

"I'm glad my movements are providing entertainment for the tittle-tattlers," Ralph said with derision.

"Got to know everything about potential opponents, my boy. Doesn't do to go into a game blind."

"You'd be surprised how many do," Ralph said.

"Aye, and that's why your pockets are bulging. Challenge me one night and you might not be so fortunate," Lord Hoylake promised.

"I'll keep that in mind." Ralph nodded as the earl left him, once he was sure there was no opportunity to try and fleece the younger man.

Settling into an ox-blood chair, Ralph placed his glass down and got out his snuff box. Flipping the lid, he took a pinch out of the exquisitely engraved silver box.

"Don't let Brummell, or his cronies, see you using two hands to open your snuff box," came the laughing voice of Miles. "You'd be ostracised as being not quite the thing."

"Thankfully, he won't be able to see me from Calais," Ralph responded.

Miles sat in the chair recently occupied by Lord Hoylake. "It's good to see you, but what brings you here?"

"I don't honestly know," Ralph admitted. "An unusual reluctance to return home."

"That's unlike you. I've usually the devil of a task to get you out anywhere."

"I've been feeling a tad restless these last few days. Don't know what the deuce has come over me, but I hope it doesn't last!"

Miles smiled. "Is now a good time to persuade you to join my sister and myself on a ride to Highgate tomorrow? Edith has a desire to explore some of the parkland around there. We could make a day of it and enjoy some refreshments at the Castle Inn. It's a respectable establishment."

"I don't think spending a day with your sister would be a good idea. We nearly came to blows after ten minutes," Ralph said.

"She's quite harmless when you get to know her," Miles defended his sister.

"A high recommendation indeed!" Ralph mocked. "Thank you for the offer, but I'd best be thinking of returning to my estate again." And what faces me there, he thought bleakly.

"You are fastidious in your care," Miles complimented him. "I feel quite the absent landlord in comparison."

"My estate is closer to London than yours," Ralph said quickly. "It makes more sense for me to keep a check on what's going on."

"That's why we have stewards, dear boy," Miles lectured with a grin. "Why employ someone and then do all the work yourself? That's not good economics."

"So, you've turned into the worst type of absent landlord," Ralph countered. "Shame on you."

"I am unrepentant. In fact, I'm even worse, for I intend to browbeat you until you succumb to my coaxing and join us tomorrow. How can you resist my company for a whole day? You know you want to!"

Ralph paused. He did want to spend a day in which he would not be required to think, to prepare, or to react to any of his responsibilities. He couldn't remember the last time he'd had a day like that.

"I'll join you," he said.

"Really? That was easier than expected!" Miles said with pleasure. "Come to Curzon Street at eleven."

"I'll be there at noon. I'm not getting out of bed early for anyone," Ralph retorted.

Miles grinned. "That's capital! I hadn't expected to set off before one."

"I didn't have you down for such a slyboots. You won't get me so easily next time!"

*

Ralph knew he should have been late. Miles was dallying, probably fussing over his cravat if past experience was anything to go by, Ralph fulminated silently. He stood before the grand marble fireplace in the drawing room of the house. Silence had descended in the room and time was dragging interminably.

Edith was seated, resplendent in her rich blue military-style riding habit with contrasting black braiding and watching Ralph with apprehension. He was certainly fine to look at, his clothes fitted him to perfection. There was no padding of the shoulders or calves, nor was there a corset holding in a rounded stomach; he was broad shouldered and lean. The material he wore was of the finest quality and his cravat tumbled in the nonchalant way that only the most talented nonpareils could achieve. Unfortunately for Edith, being in company with a handsome man didn't necessarily mean the conversation would flow easily. They had made stilted attempts to converse for the last twenty minutes and both were wishing themselves miles away. It didn't bode well for the day ahead.

Lady Longdon surprised them both by bursting into the room. "Edith! What is the meaning of this?" she cried, not acknowledging Ralph's presence, or possibly not even noticing he was there in her hurry to accost her daughter.

"I don't understand what you mean, Mama. I'm waiting with Lord Pensby for Miles to join us. We're going to Highbury," Edith explained, trying to bring to her mother's attention that they had a guest.

"No. No. Not that," Lady Longdon dismissed her daughter's words. "This." She held out a poorly wrapped parcel to her daughter. "I have just been accosted on my own doorstep by a delivery boy, who winked at me! WINKED at me as he handed this parcel to me. Why are you receiving a parcel full of letters, Edith?"

"Oh dear God," Edith muttered, but loud enough for Ralph to hear. The colour drained from her cheeks, leaving behind a deathlike pallor. "Mama, let me take them from you."

"You will do no such thing without giving me an explanation first," Lady Longdon responded tartly, pulling the parcel out of Edith's grasp.

Edith and Ralph watched in awed wonder as the sudden motion of Lady Longdon caused the already ripped wrapping paper to split and the letters to leave the confines of the parcel in an arc of paper. It seemed the letters floated to the ground, in an effort to ensure the observers were fully aware of what the parcel contained.

A moment of stillness descended on the room before Edith sprang into action, frenziedly gathering the letters. She turned a deep crimson with shame when silently, Ralph handed her a pile he'd gathered unobtrusively.

"Thank you," she muttered. "Please excuse me."

Leaving the room and running blindly up the stairs, her progress was stayed by Miles who was about to descend. "What's the commotion about?" her brother asked.

"I can't come out today. I can't show my face ever again! What was I thinking?" Edith moaned.

"Edith, this is not like you. Come. What is the matter?" Miles saw what she grasped in her hands and groaned. "Mother's seen the letters?" he asked.

Edith tried to blink the moisture away in her eyes. "Yes. The delivery boy gave the parcel to her. It was torn and when I tried to get it… Lord Pensby…" She felt almost hysterical at the thought of what their guest had seen.

"Don't worry about Ralph, he's too much of a gentleman to mention anything. You are going to get a scolding off mother, once she realises what's been going on," Miles cautioned.

"He might be a gentleman, but I know he's seen them! What must he think?" Edith said. "I can't go out. Please send my apologies, although he won't expect to see me after this, I'm sure."

Miles thought it prudent not to mention that Ralph would know exactly what the letters were. "No. You are joining us, or you will spend the day being reprimanded by mother. Get rid of those letters and meet us on the pavement in five minutes. I've sent word to bring the horses round."

After a moment's pause Edith nodded her acquiescence. Miles was right. Better to face the embarrassment of being in Ralph's company than listen to the recriminations of her mother, which were going to be long and protracted.

"Just one other thing, Edith," Miles waited until Edith met his gaze. "This has to stop. It's a recipe for disaster. It always was and I was foolish in indulging you. When you return, you will write to *The Times* and cancel your advertisement. The risk to your reputation can't be borne. Today has proved how you've been dallying with folly."

Edith didn't argue. She just nodded her head once more and continued up the stairs to her chamber.

*

The threesome allowed their horses to expel some energy once they'd cleared the busy streets of the city. There was little time for talking, for which Edith was grateful. Only general chat was exchanged as they approached Highbury, but when they reached the Castle Inn, Miles was fussing over his horse, so Ralph led Edith into a private parlour.

"My lord, about this morning..." Edith started, needing to say some words about the horrific incident.

"You've no need to explain anything to me. It isn't my concern after all," Ralph responded, taking his gloves off and walking to the fire to warm his hands.

"It must seem a little odd." Edith didn't know what to say, but she was compelled to try and explain.

"For all I know, you are heavily in debt and all your creditors decided, on the same day, to approach you for recompense," Ralph said easily, unaccountably not wishing to prolong the distress Edith was suffering.

Laughing despite her embarrassment, Edith sat down. "You have guessed correctly. I'm a shameful woman, my lord."

Unable to stop himself smiling in return, Ralph turned slightly to her. "I guessed the moment we were reacquainted. I shall have to take you to one of my gaming hells and watch you sink further as you try and pay off what you owe. It's what those in debt do regularly."

"My talents are sadly lacking in that area. I would likely come out with even more problems than I entered with."

"Most people do."

"But not you?" Edith was compelled to ask.

"No."

"I don't know why, but you don't strike me as a gambler. I suppose you don't have the air of a man who is reliant on the turn of a card," Edith admitted, completely distracted from her own mortification.

Ralph couldn't help the chuckle escaping. "You certainly don't hesitate in giving your opinions, Lady Edith."

Edith flushed, but smiled. "You laugh at my forwardness, but I became overly defensive of yours. You must wonder at my inconsistent and antagonistic behaviour."

"Your words do not offend me. But to get back to your original statement, I'm not a man who is reliant on what others consider lady luck. I gamble for another reason," Ralph admitted.

"Is there another reason other than to win funds?"

"In my case there is. Winning the funds is a pleasant consequence of the activity but the main attraction is that for those minutes of the game, I am completely focused on what is happening in front of me. I have to concentrate wholeheartedly. For those few moments nothing else intrudes and that is worth risking losing some blunt, if I do," Ralph explained.

Edith frowned slightly as she thought through his words. "I won't question as to why you need to block out everything so wholly, although I admit to wishing to know," she smiled. "I don't forget how this conversation started and I thank you for your consideration."

Ralph nodded. "As no one else knows my motivation, you hold one of my too many secrets, Lady Edith. And I now know that you're a terrible spendthrift."

Edith laughed as Miles entered the room. "Not coming to blows then?" he asked amiably. "Thought you would be after the evening at Vauxhall Gardens."

"Miles! You brute! Fancy reminding us about that disastrous event," Edith exclaimed.

"You wouldn't think I was the one needing to avoid society by that *faux pas*," Ralph said looking unperturbed.

Miles grinned. "Let's order some food. We'll have to take it slowly on our way home; I think Casper has a problem with his hind leg."

"Should you be riding him?" Edith asked.

"I'll see how he fares. If he's struggling, I'll walk him back," Miles said with a shrug.

"But it'll take hours! You'd never make it home before sundown!" Edith exclaimed.

"Better that than ruin my horse. I might have to leave him here and hire a hack, which I'll be loath to do. Probably better to be safe than sorry, I suppose," Miles said.

"Yes, you don't want to permanently cripple the poor beast having to carry your weight when it's under par," Ralph responded, gratified when Edith laughed at the comment.

*

The three trundled back to London after a refreshing respite. Miles soon fell behind, muttering under his breath about the inadequacies of hired horses.

"He's a spoiled cavalryman," Edith said, as the two riding thoroughbreds kept in Miles' sight but walked ahead at a slightly faster pace.

"He knows his horses though. I wouldn't buy one without his approval," Ralph admitted. He noticed her surprised look. "What have I said to astound you?" he asked with a faint smile.

Edith flushed a little. "I suppose it's the fact that you rely on someone for advice. You seem so self-assured, as most men are, I admit, but with you it's different. I suppose self-sufficient is a better description."

"I, like many others who hold the family title have to be, especially with estates to run, but I also pride myself in not being foolish either. I know I'll get a far better beast with Miles advising me. Come, even an independent woman like yourself, must seek advice sometimes."

Edith snorted in a most unladylike fashion, which made Ralph laugh. "You would think, being of age and having my own fortune would open the world to me, would you not? Instead, I feel almost as constrained as I did when I was in the schoolroom. I'm very much forced to bow to the wishes of my mother and even my brother in some instances," Edith said bitterly.

"We all have restrictions in our lives, even as the head of the family," Ralph reasoned.

"I suppose you do," Edith admitted. "But I do think being a woman, even a rich one is different to the situation of a man. I wish to return to the country, but my brother and mother wish differently, so I have no option other than to stay in the city. They doubt I know my own mind, which is devilishly frustrating."

"You really want to leave whilst the season is in full swing?" Ralph asked in surprise. He'd been given a hint of Edith's character from Miles, but hearing her own views was fascinating.

"Yes. I'm an ungrateful brat, I realise that, even if my mother hadn't told me the same, albeit in slightly more polite terms," Edith said ruefully.

Ralph laughed again. "You surprise me, Lady Edith. I thought dancing, flirting and refusing proposals was the highlight of a young woman's come-out."

"You make us sound positively fickle and shallow!" Edith exclaimed. "Yet, you have no recriminations for the men who offer for three women in one week. Surely that can't be seen as good *ton*?"

"No? Really? Which buffoon did that? And dare I ask, were you number one, two or three?" Ralph asked, barely suppressing the chuckle which threatened to emerge.

Glowering, Edith huffed. "I was number three."

"Don't worry. That sentence alone has persuaded me that the man is a complete fool," Ralph said seriously.

"Thank you. I admit, even if I'd been number one, there wouldn't have been an acceptance given. He wasn't refused out of my being piqued," Edith admitted.

"I would hope not. It does reassure me that I'm not missing anything by my remaining on the outskirts of society."

"It surprises me that you do. A single, handsome man is always popular."

"Good to know that you consider me handsome," Ralph said with a chuckle.

Although Edith's cheeks flamed, she smiled. "You know full well you are. My admitting something so obvious, is not my flirting with you, my lord."

"I apologise that I dared to presume such a thing," Ralph replied, his lips twitching at the glare his words caused. He paused a moment before continuing. "I choose not to go into society because I can never marry."

"Oh? Can't or won't?"

"And you accused me of impertinence!" Ralph laughed. "Now don't glare daggers at me, I only tease you. To answer your question, it's a bit of both, Lady Edith. Does that satisfy your curiosity?"

"Of course not! But I am lady enough not to probe further."

"What a disappointment!" Ralph mocked gently.

"By all that is ungentlemanly!" Edith laughed. "You, sir, are a rogue."

"It has been said before a time or two."

Edith glanced sideways, wondering about the enigmatic gentleman who seemed to have many layers. Oh, their start had been tetchy, but she was intrigued and certainly attracted to him. Still wondering what was behind his comment about not marrying, she could admit to feeling that it was a shame that he wasn't on the marriage mart. For the first time in her life she felt she had met someone who she was drawn to, who attracted her mentally and physically. Perhaps he could be persuaded to change his outlook on the matrimonial state if he met the right woman? She felt a frisson of excitement. It was worth spending more time with him, especially as she'd come into contact with him due to his friendship with Miles.

      Suddenly, the season in London wasn't looking quite so bleak.

Chapter 5

Ralph left Curzon Street with confused feelings. He'd put Edith down, after their first disastrous meeting, as a virago, but since then…

Knowing about the letters had given him an advantage to understand what had mortified her that morning, but there was something else. He had wanted to reassure her, to relieve her of her embarrassment when they'd stopped at the inn. What was even stranger, was his need to explain to her why he didn't consider himself the gamester that others would. He'd never told a soul about finding temporary relief at the gaming tables, not even Miles.

It had been a refreshing day. Not for a long time had he spent hours not dwelling on his problems. Instead he'd enjoyed the company of an amusing, beautiful woman. He couldn't remember a time he'd laughed so much. It had felt good.

He was still pondering on why he'd been so open as he entered his own address. He rented a small house on Jermyn Street. There was no need for anything larger as there would only ever be himself visiting the capital.

Being helped out of his exquisitely fitted frock coat, his valet cleared his throat. "A letter was delivered today from Lymewood, my lord."

"Blast it," Ralph muttered. "Where is it?"

He was handed the missive, sent from his steward at his family home. Reading it through he sucked in a breath at what he read. *There have been three attacks these last two days, my lord. The recovery from those incidents has been slow and full of confusion and distress. It seems the ongoing treatment doesn't appear to be working.*

"Wilson, I will be returning to Lymewood on the morrow. I shall send an express immediately advising them of my plans," Ralph said, sitting at his small desk and reaching for his pen, all thoughts of an enjoyable day forgotten.

*

Edith entered her bedchamber with feelings of apprehension. She had enjoyed a good day, but was also curious about the letters which had been delivered.

Her maid helped her out of her riding habit and fixed her hair to get rid of the effects of a day's riding. Only then was she able to dismiss the maid and be alone. She immediately crossed to the top drawer in her tallboy and lifted out the jumbled pile of letters.

Sitting next to the welcome warming fire, she started to open each letter. Ten minutes later and the fire was burning brighter than it had been a few moments previously, as Edith placed one piece of paper on top of the other. Her eyes were overly bright as she realised her plan had come to naught.

The last one to be burned was the second letter from the correspondent who had written to her in the first batch she'd received. The first letter had seemed to be promising, but the second letter was an utter disappointment. *With your dowry and my ideas, we shall want for nothing. I am sure the schemes I have agreed to enter into when we make out connection official will bear fruit, my dear lady. I will be able to offer you everything your heart desires and more. All I need is the funds to start off and I'm sure your independence will provide that. It is providence that I chose to read the personal advertisements that very day. We were destined to be together, I'm sure of it.* The letter had read.

On rereading the missive, Edith almost growled. "I might have been foolish to mention I was independent, but that's where my stupidity ends, Mr Penny," she muttered to the paper. "If you think I'm handing over my fortune for you to squander, you picked the wrong girl! Providence indeed! You probably write to every person who places an advertisement. Shame on you, sir," she finished, screwing the letter up before throwing it roughly into the fire.

Getting up from her chair, she walked across to the window. Wrapping her arms around her middle she gazed out onto the small gardens and the backs of other houses. "There must be someone out there for me, surely? In all these houses, in this huge city, how can there not be one man who I can love and respect? Am I so difficult to please?"

Unbidden, an image of Ralph came to her mind. She smiled slightly to herself. "He's certainly handsome and there's more to him than would first appear. A pity he can be taciturn and abrupt." Her words didn't affect the smile on her face, in fact it increased as she thought over her day.

Yes. Lord Pensby was the bright spot in a very lonely city.

*

Edith entered the drawing room, a smile on her face. Miles glanced at his sister.

"You're looking pretty, have you done something different?" he asked. "You look younger somehow."

"Such a typical brother, issuing a compliment at the same time as a thinly veiled insult," Edith said, raising her eyebrows.

"Not at all. Just pointing out your efforts haven't been wasted."

Edith rolled her eyes at this remark. "I've done something that will make you happy," she changed the subject.

"Oh?"

"I've been through the latest letters and you'll be reassured to know that I won't be writing to any of the correspondents. It seems you were right, an advertisement wasn't the way to find a life partner," she admitted. "In fact, I've burned them all."

"Thank God for that!" Miles responded vehemently. "I've been having nightmares about it since you sent the details to the paper."

"I've sent a note through, asking for the advertisement to be removed," Edith admitted. "It was worth a try, but no one caught my attention in truth. A little depressing when there are so many advertisements placed."

"There are never any announcements to say that the couple who are to marry met through the paper itself. If that was the case, they'd be sure to promote the fact, it would encourage more desperate people to send their details in."

"I'm glad to know what you think of me, but I do wish you'd learn some more flowery phrases. There is no need to be quite so brutal, you know," Edith huffed.

Miles smiled. "Come, my dear, I promise to be the most delightful brother at the ball tonight. I will even accompany you into supper so you don't have to deal with mother alone."

"You are all kindness," Edith responded sarcastically.

*

Ralph didn't attend balls, Edith knew that, but it didn't stop her from scanning the ballroom to see if he'd had a change of heart. She'd hoped that their afternoon together might have tempted him to join them, hoping that he'd felt the stirrings as she had.

Miles interrupted her musings by coming across to her. "Edith, I'd like to introduce these two gentlemen to you. They've only just arrived in London. Albert Malone served with me in Spain and France and he's here with his friend, Charles Sage."

Edith smiled and curtseyed at the two gentlemen. "Mr Malone, Mr Sage, it's a pleasure to meet you."

Both gentlemen bowed. Charles spoke first. "Lady Edith, I hope you have a dance spare, I am keen to make up for time lost spent travelling through Europe to reach London."

"I have the next with Miles, but if he has no objection, I'm happy to change partners."

Miles nodded his acquiescence. "It'll give me a good opportunity to catch up with Albert," he said.

"Not too long though for reminiscing. I would also like to dance with Lady Edith, if it is at all possible?"

"Of course," Edith smiled.

She walked through the crowded room to the dance floor with Charles at her side. He was the more handsome of the pair, with blond locks and clear blue eyes. He looked almost angelic, and his unruly curls just added to the overall striking effect. He attracted a few admiring glances as they took their places, at which Edith suppressed a smile. She could appreciate dancing with a handsome partner, like any other woman could.

Honouring each other as the dance started, Charles soon showed he was a light-footed dancer, who could entertain as well as spring through the steps.

"My friend speaks highly of your brother," he started.

"That's nice to know. I believe he was a well thought of officer. Did Mr Malone serve under Wellington?"

"Yes, in the Peninsular and then France," Charles said. "I'm afraid I wasn't brave enough to purchase a commission."

The comment was said without the slightest doubt that his words would be censured and his presumption was correct.

"It isn't a lifestyle which suits everyone," Edith said. "I know my brother misses the bond he shared with his fellow men, but I'm sure there is much of his experience he would rather forget."

"Yet we shouldn't be allowed to, because of the sacrifice those brave boys gave," Charles said as they twirled a full turn.

"Quite. Have you been travelling, as you haven't been here for the full season?"

"Yes. My friend wanted his memories of the continent to be happy ones, so wished to visit France, Spain and Portugal now they aren't being ravaged by war. I was willing to accompany him, as I hadn't travelled on my grand tour because of the troubles. Missing the start of the season seemed a small price to pay so Albert could have company on his journey," Charles explained.

"You must have seen some beautiful places," Edith responded, a little longing in her voice.

"I have. The churches over there are something to behold. Gold everywhere. Far more extravagant than ours."

"I suppose they are mostly Catholic?"

"Yes, they are. Still very pretty to look at. Although all that Latin is beyond me. I'm afraid I wasn't a good scholar when my parents employed tutors for me. I was more interested in riding horses and flirting with young ladies."

Edith laughed. "And what did the young ladies think of this?"

Charles smiled boyishly. "Oh, they didn't mind overly much. But I can assure you, I'm far more respectable these days."

Edith was thus entertained through the half hour. Her cheeks were aching because of laughing at the end of it and then she was dancing with Albert, who tried to be as charming as Charles had, but his quieter demeanour couldn't compete with the gregarious Charles. After their dance had finished, Edith took Albert's offered arm.

"Would you like to join me in a glass of lemonade, or punch, Lady Edith?"

"That would be lovely, thank you," Edith said. "It is extremely hot in here."

They manoeuvred their way through the crowded ballroom. The hostess, with two marriageable daughters, would consider the event a great success. Her rooms were bursting with people intent on having a good night before moving on to the next party, or other entertainment, of the evening.

Edith and Albert eventually reached the slightly less crowded refreshment room and after pulling out a seat for Edith, Albert obtained two glasses of homemade lemonade.

Edith drank gratefully. "Thank you for this, it was a good idea."

"You're welcome and it delays my handing you over to your next partner," Albert said, joining her at the small table.

"I have no other dances until after supper," Edith admitted.

"You surprise me. I thought there would be no chance of spending any time with you this evening. A fortunate circumstance on my part to find out my presumption was wrong."

Edith smiled. "I think my penchant for caustic comments puts off the more delicate partners I have previously danced with."

"Ah, so you are very like your brother then," Albert smiled as Edith laughed.

"He would have me think he's the popular one," Edith countered.

"Oh, that's very true, the handsome charmer that he is, but he can't help his words sometimes. Gets him into all sorts of trouble."

"I shall remind him of that the next time he offers me a set-down for not pausing before I utter what I'm thinking."

Albert smiled. "I shall be forewarned in case your words are aimed at me. I'm glad to be in contact again with your brother, especially in a happier situation."

"Yes. Mr Sage explained that you needed a holiday before returning home."

"Oh. Yes. I did," Albert said, a little discomfited. "Seems fanciful, but I feel better coming back now."

"I often wonder how any of you can make a return to society and appear normal. I'm not sure I could," Edith admitted.

"You have to carry on. For the sake of the ones who were lost if nothing else."

"Shall we see a lot more of you now, or are you still intent on travelling?" Edith asked. She had immediately been drawn to the two gentlemen and would be glad to spend more time in their company. They didn't attract her like Ralph had done, that had been something she'd never experienced previously, but it was pleasant to spend time in company she could enjoy.

"No. We are both to stay for the rest of the season, so expect many dances, Lady Edith."

"I shall look forward to it."

*

It was too much to expect that Lady Longdon hadn't noticed the newcomers and the fact they had spent time with her daughter. As soon as the coach had started on their homeward journey, she turned to Edith.

"Mr Malone and Mr Sage seem like fine gentlemen and appeared taken with you. Two dances with each shows promise for the future," she started without preamble.

Edith swallowed a retort because Lady Longdon would curse her daughter for being so abrupt and unwilling to encourage two new gentlemen. She just saved her breath and the inevitable scolding which would follow such a foolish response.

"They say they are good friends of Miles'," she responded, looking to her brother to distract their mother.

"I know Malone, but Sage is a newcomer to me," Miles admitted. "Seems a pleasant enough fellow and will certainly be a hit with the ladies with his good looks."

"Two handsome gentlemen. Both beautifully dressed. Although Mr Sage is by far the more striking," Lady Longdon confessed.

"He is," Edith admitted. "But Mr Malone is very pleasant. Perhaps not as outwardly confident as Mr Sage, but I enjoyed talking to him in the refreshment room." Mr Malone had dark blond hair and green eyes, which by contrast to Mr Sage, could never really compete. Even the most hardened of females couldn't fail to see the beauty in the cherubic looks of the young man.

"We must plan an entertainment in which they can be guests of honour," Lady Longdon said.

"I don't think either would expect such a gesture," Miles said, his eyes laughing at Edith's stony expression.

"Even more reason to do it," Lady Longdon insisted.

Edith knew there was no point in arguing against her mother when she had an idea fixed in her head and if there was a chance of a proposal, Lady Longdon would do all she could to advance the scheme. "I hope you'll also invite Lord Pensby, as he's also a friend of Miles."

"Ralph is out of town," Miles said.

"Oh? But he was only with us yesterday and mentioned nothing of leaving," Edith said, disappointment clear in her voice.

Miles narrowed his eyes at his sister. "He'd mentioned about returning home. I persuaded him to delay his departure, but then I received a note to say he'd had to leave London suddenly. I've no idea when he returns."

"Singular that he departs in the middle of the season," Lady Longdon said.

"He explains it that he doesn't live that far out of town and he doesn't really take part in everything London has to offer anyway," Miles explained. "I think there are some family issues though."

"Do you not know what they are?" Edith asked.

"No. He hasn't offered an explanation and I'm certainly not asking him," Miles said. "Not everyone wants to furnish the tittle-tattlers with the latest *on dit*."

"I wouldn't expect that to happen. You are his friend. Surely he would wish to confide in you?" Edith persisted.

"No. Sometimes it's easier to keep things to oneself."

Edith wondered if Miles was referring to himself as well as Ralph but stopped questioning her brother. She was unaccountably disappointed that Ralph had left town and she hadn't known.

Lady Longdon filled the journey home with plans for a dinner she would hold, suggesting menus and guests with very little input from either of her children. There was no need for their participation as she was quite focused on what she thought were the best dishes and who she considered the best guests. She spent a happy half hour planning her grand event.

Entering into the house, Lady Longdon immediately requested to see the cook.

"Mama, you cannot at this hour!" Edith exclaimed at her mother's words.

"I need to make sure there is time to prepare," Lady Longdon insisted.

"I doubt anything will be lost between now and tomorrow morning, except the poor woman's sleep," Edith insisted.

Miles intervened before his mother could retort to his sister. "She's right, Mama. Tomorrow morning will be a perfect time to plan. Then you will have all day to see cook and the housekeeper. Off to bed with you now, my lovely," he said, kissing his mother's cheek.

Lady Longdon smiled at her son. "You're right of course. I am feeling a little tired. I shall go straight to bed and start issuing instructions tomorrow. Edith, you will write the invitations under my guidance."

"Yes, Mama," came the dutiful response.

Miles and Edith waited until their mother had ascended the stairs, at which point Edith turned to her brother. "I have no idea how you manage to turn her to your will as easily as you do, but I wish I had that talent," Edith said.

"She expects an argument from you, you should try to be more persuasive than confrontational," Miles said with a grin as they followed in their mother's wake.

"Beast!" Edith responded tartly.

"See? I rest my case," Miles grinned, before becoming serious. "Edith, what are your plans with regards to Ralph?"

"I don't know what you mean," Edith said, hoping her cheeks weren't betraying her by flushing guiltily.

"You seemed very keen on him being invited to the party and then almost distraught on hearing he'd left town."

"Oh, poppycock! You have a vivid imagination, brother! He's your friend and I like him, nothing else," Edith said defensively.

"I hope that's all it is, for I would hate for you to choose Ralph as the one to have affection for. It won't end happily if that's the case," Miles cautioned.

"I'm not going to develop anything for anyone," Edith lied. "But why would it have such a poor end? What is wrong with him? I thought he was your friend."

"He is. I like him a lot, but he is troubled and a troubled man doesn't equate to a happy husband."

"In that case, it's a good thing I won't be setting my cap at him. He told me himself – in a more general conversation before you start to panic – that he wasn't the marrying kind," Edith said airily, separating from her brother at the top of the stairs. She turned down the landing towards her own room, leaving Miles to continue to his own room alone.

"You'd best listen to him, Edith," Miles said quietly, before she was out of earshot. "Damaged men aren't a good bet."

Edith flashed Miles a look of concern, but her brother had already turned away from her. Once more she felt that Miles was talking more about himself than anyone else.

Chapter 6

Ralph entered the room, after quietly scratching on the door. The air seemed still it was so quiet inside. The nurse acknowledged his presence with a slight nod of the head and rose to approach him.

"How is she?" Ralph asked, looking at the bundle on the bed.

"She's been very tired and confused," came the quiet answer. "The doctor has given her a course of laudanum to keep her quiet, but he's constantly asking to take her into hospital for tests."

"He wants to lock her away in the asylum," Ralph said roughly.

"Yes," the nurse admitted. "He says all patients with similar symptoms fare better there."

"My mother isn't becoming a medical experiment. Not whilst I have breath in my body," Ralph said.

"I've told him your opinion, but I'm sure he'll want to speak to you again when he calls tomorrow."

Ralph nodded his head and moved over to the bedside. "I'll sit with her," he said, sitting down on the wooden chair.

The nurse left the pair alone. It was a well-practised routine. Ralph would barely leave his mother's side until she reached some sort of normality, then he would eventually return to London, only to be brought back when needed.

The only reason he travelled to London was because the attacks would happen whether or not he was present and he had to maintain his own sanity, if he was to be his mother's protector. Added to that, it distressed her to think she was holding him back, so in many ways it was easier to go when she begged him to.

Reaching over, he found his mother's hand in the bundle of blankets which covered her. He took the thin limb and kissed it before placing it once more on the bed, but this time in his gentle hold. They remained like that for hours, until eventually, Lady Pensby stirred.

"Ralph?" she asked croakily.

"I'm here, Mother."

"I thought they'd send for you. I'm sorry."

"What for, dearest? You think I'd rather stay in London than be with you when you're unwell?"

"You have a life to live. You don't need me holding you back."

Ralph reached over and kissed his mother's forehead. "I have all that I need here. You just concentrate on resting. You know it helps."

"I detest laudanum," came the drowsy response.

"I know, but it lets your body rest. You'll soon not need it and be back to normal."

"I feel so drained, Ralph."

"I'm sorry you feel so. Close your eyes and sleep, my dearest. I'll be here when you awake," Ralph promised. The lump in his throat was hard to swallow, but he remained still until his mother's breathing was steady and rhythmic.

Ringing the bell, to alert the nurse he was leaving his mother's bedchamber, Ralph went to freshen up in his own set of rooms. From experience he knew he would have a few hours before there would be any further signs of consciousness and he used the time to meet with his steward and housekeeper.

The old retainer welcomed him as she always did. "It's good to see you, Master Ralph."

Ralph wondered what age he would be before his childhood title would be dropped by the woman who'd known him since he was born. "What happened this time?" he asked, knowing he would receive an honest, succinct response.

"The first one seemed to come out of nowhere. She was writing at her desk in her parlour and the next thing she'd collapsed. Luckily there was a housemaid in the room and we could react quickly. I'm afraid the second and third time occurred whilst she was in her bed. That's something new."

Ralph frowned. "It is. Had laudanum been given?"

"Yes, but the doctor increased the dose afterwards. You'll have noticed she seems groggier than normal."

"She was lucid when she spoke."

"Good. She hasn't been until today, but I think that was more the effect of the laudanum, rather than the illness."

"I hope so," Ralph admitted.

"The doctor will be here soon," the housekeeper advised.

"I'll see him in the study," Ralph said, standing to leave the room. "He'd better not come out with his usual rot."

The housekeeper chose not to comment; she knew exactly what the doctor would say. He'd been making the same request for the last couple of years.

Ralph entered his study and went straight to the decanters on the side table. Pouring himself a large measure, he took a substantial mouthful of brandy before looking around the room. This room reminded him of his father and helped to support him in some unknown way. His father had refused to abandon his mother to the doctor's ministrations and Ralph was determined to do the same.

Within the hour the doctor was ushered into the well-ordered room. Sitting at the chair on the opposite side of the large oak desk at which Ralph was seated, he started to speak.

"It's been a bad week for Lady Pensby," the doctor said.

"I believe so. Are there no new treatments?" Ralph asked.

"We have yet to try the treatments available in the asylum. She would be well cared for I can assure you."

"You want to drill holes into her brain. I will not consent to that, nor will she. Ever," Ralph ground out.

"But if it relieves the pressure in her brain…"

"You can give me no guarantees that the treatment will work, or that she'll survive the procedure. I will never give my consent. Try your butchering on some other poor soul, my mother is out of bounds."

"But, my lord—"

"You can 'my lord' as much as you wish. I pay you an exorbitant amount of money to ease her symptoms and keep her comfortable. At the moment all I can see you are doing is increasing the dose of laudanum, which can't be good for her in the long term," Ralph said.

"No, it isn't," the doctor admitted. "But I have little else to offer."

"Then perhaps I need to look for someone who has."

A look of alarm crossed the medical man's face before he masked his expression. Ralph knew it was because if he lost the patronage of the Pensbys his income would reduce to probably less than half its current amount. "No! I shall seek advice from my peers and explore more medical journals. I will try to find an alternative."

"Whatever you find, be assured that I will only agree to it, if it can be administered at home," Ralph said.

"That does limit our options, but I will do what I can," the doctor said, rising from his chair. "I hope to see you again before you return to London."

"I shall be here for as long as my mother needs me," Ralph stated brusquely.

*

Eating alone in the large dining room, Ralph dismissed the staff. He didn't need the butler and two footmen to attend to his needs when he could reach every dish and had the wine decanter at his elbow.

As the door closed softly behind the banished servants, Ralph gazed around the room. Had it ever enjoyed the number of parties a room of this size would normally, he mused. As far back as he could remember, his family's life had been quieter than other aristocratic families had. There had been an almost innate understanding that his mother required a quiet, uneventful life.

He didn't begrudge that his childhood was less frivolous than those of his peers. He was more inclined to be on the fringes of any group. Whether it was because of his upbringing, or purely his own nature, he neither knew nor cared. He was who he was and he had no inclination to change.

He only wished that his mother could find some form of release which didn't require her to be locked in an asylum. He knew it was her biggest fear and his father had promised his wife and then made his son promise his mother, that she would never be admitted to one of those hellish places.

When Ralph's father had been alive, they'd gone to visit one of the establishments to see what was on offer. He was told that his mother had suffered nightmares for a month afterwards and her terrors had only ended when she was given assurances time and again, that she wouldn't be forced to enter any such institution.

He rubbed his fingers across his forehead, as if that could massage away the permanent frown lines which marred his features. It seemed a long time ago that he'd allowed Miles to persuade him to join the trip to Highbury. He should have returned home as he'd planned and he would struggle with the guilt caused by the decision he'd made, but he'd enjoyed himself. A rare day out with good company and pleasant surroundings.

Sighing, he stood and walked out of the dining room, returning to his study. He took out a cigar from a locked box in his desk. Miles had introduced him to the alternative to snuff when he'd returned from the Peninsular, but they were still expensive enough when shipping them from Spain, that they were kept for a special occasion.

Ralph considered the evening to be enough of an excuse to light one.

Using a taper to get a flame from the fire, he puffed until the end of the cigar glowed red. Throwing the taper into the fire, he seated himself in the large brown leather chair and crossing his feet at the ankles he stretched out, gazing into the fire.

One person intruded into his thoughts. He found her exasperating, beautiful and entertaining at the same time.

He shouldn't be thinking of her. She had made no secret of the fact that she wanted to marry and he couldn't offer that to anyone. How could he allow himself to become close to someone, to plan a future, when he never knew what would happen with his mother? He could never force his mother to live anywhere else, other than in the home she'd known since her marriage at eighteen. Here she was surrounded by staff who cared for her. No new bride would risk having the previous mistress still living under the same roof. That's what Dower Houses were built for.

No. Considering a future with someone else was selfish on his part. He had to focus on his mother and hope that they found, in time, if not a cure, something to ease her suffering.

Unable to remain seated, he prowled the room. "If I know what I need to do, why is it so blasted hard this time?" he muttered as he walked. "She's foolish anyway. Who would consider advertising in a newspaper to try and attract a husband? The silly chit." He would never understand why Miles hadn't found a way of stopping his sister.

Ralph couldn't shake the connection they'd shared though. She had been so easy to talk to. He stood near his desk. It would be good to talk over his worries with someone. He'd never done that, not even with Miles and he trusted him implicitly.

He couldn't talk to Edith though. He had no idea when he was returning to London. She could be married by then for all he knew and then there could definitely be no in-depth chats, for he wasn't one who coveted another man's wife. The thought of her being wed depressed him, but he shook it off.

Taking out a piece of parchment, he dipped his quill into his ink stand. There was one way he could speak to her and even if she didn't reply, he would feel better for expressing the words.

    He started to scratch the pen across the paper.

Chapter 7

Edith laughed as the horses pounded over the heathland, hot breath being snorted out as they let their hooves fly. The group moved like a single, disjointed beast, travelling fast over the undulating ground.

Eventually, their speed slowed and the riders congratulated each other on their animals' prowess. Edith smiled at Miss King, one of the six riders in the group.

"Your horse is fabulous, Susan!" she said, reigning her own beast in to trot alongside the young woman. "I'm quite jealous."

"My father probably paid too much for him, but I am pleased I have him. He is the best horse I've ever ridden," came the proud response.

"I can believe it," Edith acknowledged. "It was a good idea of Mr Malone's to come on the heath. Hyde Park just doesn't offer the space to really gallop."

"Oh no! Too many people to go above a gentle trot. I don't usually take Star out when I'm going to the park. It seems wrong to restrain him so," Susan admitted.

"You are right. By the way, I meant to ask, have you seen that Mr Chumley is to marry? Miles told me of the announcement in *The Times* this morning," Edith said.

"Yes. I feel we both had a lucky escape. I do feel sorry for Miss Williams, but she is of an age to make her own decisions. It was no secret that he'd proposed to all three of us in the same week."

"It is hard to be harsh on one of our sex, but she must be desperate indeed to have accepted him. She, like us, must be aware of his reputation," Edith said.

"She is seven and twenty though. It is a good match in many respects I suppose," Susan reasoned. She had been best friends with Edith for years and very often was the voice of reason to Edith's more spirited nature. If Edith considered herself handsome, but far from beautiful, Susan was prone to consider herself as plain. An unfortunate stepfamily had ensured the lack of confidence of a shy young girl was used against the child to boost the family's feelings of superiority, whilst harming Susan's impression of herself.

"I hope I'm never in the position that I'm forced to consider a man like Mr Chumley is my best option," Edith said tartly.

A chuckle behind the pair, made them aware that their comments had been overheard and both looked a little chagrined.

"Lady Edith, I would take out a wager if it was *de rigueur* to do so, on the fact that you won't ever be put in such a situation," Mr Sage said.

Edith blushed. "That is very kind of you to say, but my words were uncouth. Please forget I uttered them; I shouldn't be so unkind."

"As you wish, but I stand by what I said. Both of you shall not want for eligible men knocking on your doors."

"As I've reached the ripe old age of three and twenty, I can honestly say I shall turn into an old maid before that happens," Edith laughed. "But Miss King, I've heard, does have a regular posse of beaux desperate to gain her affection."

This time it was Susan's turn to laugh. "My dowry is what they covet, not my charms, and before you accuse me of false modesty, my stepmother agrees with me. She has not seen one gentleman who favours me for my personality and not my inheritance." The peal of her stepmother's laughter if Susan ever mentioned that a young man had paid her some compliment or other had been enough to convince her of that fact.

"This is when, as a gentleman, I have to object. We cannot win when we try to court a pretty girl who is also blessed with a reasonable fortune. In that situation we are considered fortune hunters, whatever our intent is. Tell me, Miss King, Lady Edith, how are we to overcome this obstacle?" Mr Sage asked. "For I would like to know, truly."

"I think you need to find a way in which you can show your true character without coming under scrutiny," Edith said.

"That would hint at secret liaisons, which would only damage the case further," Mr Sage countered.

"Oh no! It could not be something so inappropriate. Surely there is some way of communicating what you feel without it needing to be clandestine?" Susan asked.

"I hope so," Mr Sage responded dramatically. "Or, I'm to end a very lonely man." With his words, he turned his horse and moved towards some of the others in their group.

"I think Mr Sage is smitten with you, Edith," Susan said at his retreating form. "His words were quite clear in their meaning."

"He could just have easily been talking about you, Susan," Edith said with a laugh.

"Not at all! I'm astute enough to know when a man is trying to fix my attention and Mr Sage was gazing in your direction as oft as he could."

"Could he be overwhelmed with his feelings for you and couldn't face you for fear of giving himself away?" Edith teased.

Susan burst out laughing. "You should be writing novels with such an imagination! I'm happy to be set as the romantic heroine. But as for Mr Sage, I am expecting him to try and secure you as his wife."

"He is very handsome," Edith admitted. "But as for his character – does he not seem a little flighty to you?"

"Perhaps that is what he refers to, needing to let you see his true character. Oh, I'm going to enjoy watching this romance blossom," Susan smiled in return. "It looks like your prediction of being an old maid will have no foundation after all."

*

Edith entered the ballroom on Miles' arm. She had dressed in a pale apricot gown, which added warmth to her skin tone. White flowers edged the dress and matching blossom was clipped in her hair amongst the tumble of curls. Again, she wore the diamond droplet around her neck. She had other jewellery, but always opted for the simpler pieces. Lady Longdon despaired of her daughter, claiming the *ton* would consider them close-fisted if she wore the same piece at every entertainment.

"I like this necklace," Edith had argued. "What does it matter what I wear as long as it suits my outfit and is appropriate for the event I'm attending? I'm sure people have far more interesting things to worry about, than my choice of jewellery."

"It bothers me, that should be enough to vary what you wear," Lady Longdon had snapped.

"I shall wear my pearls the next time we are out," Edith had promised meekly. Sometimes it wasn't worth the argument.

Looking around, she was aware of the faint sense of disappointment that Ralph wouldn't be attending. She had managed to casually ask Miles if he'd heard from his friend. On receiving a negative, she'd known that there would be no pleasant surprise during the evening. Her feelings were probably foolish but she'd finally met someone who had stirred something within her. A pity she looked unlikely to see him again.

Mr Sage and Mr Malone approached as soon as they saw the Longdon group.

"Lady Longdon, Lady Edith, Miles, it's good to see you all. Lady Edith, I hope you have the first two dances set aside for me," Mr Malone said, bowing over the ladies' hands.

"The dances are free, and I'll happily dance with you," Edith answered.

"You cad, Albert, I was going to ask for the first two," Mr Sage cursed his friend.

"You'll have to have the next two," Lady Edith said with a smile. "If that's acceptable?"

"Of course, I'm just repining that it will be a further hour until I can spend some time with you," Mr Sage responded, bowing over Edith's hand.

"You can accompany me instead," Miles said, amused at the verbal sparring for his sister's time. "I'm sure you'll enjoy yourself as you join me with the chaperones whilst I settle mother."

"Of course, it would be my pleasure," Mr Sage responded, looking as if he'd prefer a trip to the gallows, rather than join the chaperones.

Mr Malone chuckled at the retreating forms. "Charles would curse Miles to the devil only for your mother being in earshot."

"He could have refused Miles," Edith pointed out.

"And appear at a disadvantage in your family's eyes? Never, Lady Edith! Charles is on his best behaviour in the hope that he will impress you all."

Edith frowned slightly. Mr Malone's words suggested that Charles wasn't acting to his true character and that didn't rest easy. "There is no need to pretend he's someone he's not," she said, a little sharply.

"Come, Lady Edith! Are you trying to convince me that you act in the same way in every situation? Surely that's coming it too brown! We all behave in ways which are pertinent to what we face and who we are with," Mr Malone teased.

"I suppose so. Yes. Of course you're right," Edith admitted.

The pair danced the first two and then Edith was escorted once more onto the dance floor with Charles as her partner. She was a little reserved at the start of their dances, on which he soon picked up.

"Has my friend been such a poor partner, he has put you out of sorts, Lady Edith?" he asked with his winning smile.

"No! Not at all. Mr Malone is a very good dancer, as you are. I admit I was pondering over something he said," Edith admitted.

"Has the buffoon made a *faux pas*? I have to admit, Lady Edith, I travelled most of the continent with him going from one blunder to another. If I didn't like him so well, I'd have had to leave him in some far-off town," Charles responded as they danced.

Edith laughed. "You have a wicked sense of fun, Mr Sage."

"But does it make you smile?"

"Yes, you know it does," Edith admitted.

"Then, that's all that matters. Life would be dull if we were to be serious all of the time, don't you think?"

"Yes, it would," Edith responded. She was glad the dance separated her from her partner at that point as his words had reminded her of a pair of serious brown eyes. The memory was enough to make her colour a little and she was glad of the moment or two to bring her inner longings back under control. When the pair rejoined each other in the set, there was no outward sign on her part that her equilibrium had been upset.

When they were at the bottom of the long-ways line, standing out of the dance, Charles took hold of Edith's hands. "I hope you will allow me to express how much I enjoy your company, Lady Edith. You are an unlooked for diamond in this city. I am so glad our paths have crossed. I know my life is changed forever as a result of meeting you."

Edith pretended she needed to use her handkerchief in order to release her hands from his grasp. "Mr Sage, we hardly know each other. How can I have had such an impact in so short a time? I think you are funning me," she said, trying to keep her tone light.

"I couldn't fun when I am talking about matters of the heart. Do you not feel the same? Are my hopes and wishes to be rejected?"

"Please don't speak so," Edith said, extremely uncomfortable with the situation. She couldn't escape without causing severe offence, so had to try and stop the unwanted utterances.

"Ah, I see I speak too soon. Forgive me. I wouldn't want to frighten you with the earnestness of my feelings. I am being serious when I say how much I have been struck since meeting you, but you are correct, we are still strangers. I will work out ways of getting to know you without it feeling as if you're being put under pressure. Would that be acceptable to you?" Mr Sage said.

"I-I don't wish to give false hope," Edith started.

"All I'm asking for is a chance for you to know me better. I know there can be no guarantees," Mr Sage said, as they took their places in the set once more.

Edith was prevented from answering as they were immediately separated in the dance. Mr Sage's words had unsettled her and she wasn't convinced she'd have given a satisfactory response if they had remained together.

When the dance finally ended, she was escorted over to her mother, who had been joined by Susan, who was chatting to Miles and Albert.

Edith soon persuaded Susan to join her on a walk around the ballroom. When they found an alcove which wasn't already occupied, the two ladies sat themselves down. They were in full view of the ballroom, but at least were a little away from anyone who might overhear. Susan listened as Edith updated her on what had been exchanged with Mr Sage.

"He certainly seems to have become smitten with you very quickly, it was obvious to me he was," Susan agreed. "But I shouldn't think he should be criticised for that. You must acknowledge, he has excellent taste."

Edith laughed. "You are a good friend, Susan, but come, let's not be silly. Look at the unmarried girls in this room. Look how many beautiful, young, pleasing girls there are. I'm not foolish enough to consider myself an ape-leader, but I'm also not a diamond of the first water."

"You also have a penchant to downplay what assets you do have."

"Yet I remain unmarried."

Susan looked away, a frown marring her features.

"What is it?" Edith asked.

"Do you think you purposely put potential suitors off in some way?" the friend asked.

"I don't understand," Edith answered.

"You are very self-deprecating, which could be said is you just being overly modest, but I wonder if there is more to it than that. You dismiss the fact that someone could like you, that you are marriageable, yet you have a lot to offer. I wonder if you are purposely, subtlety somehow giving the wrong impression to anyone who's interested in you. If you don't encourage a suitor, they can interpret that as disinterest on your part and stop trying," Susan tried to explain.

"But why would I try to put eligible men off?" Edith asked, genuinely bewildered.

"Perhaps you don't really want to marry," Susan offered.

"I do. I think. No. I do," Edith smiled at her own contradictory behaviour. "For the first time I've actually met someone who has stirred something in me. Oh, I don't know if it is an attraction of the long-lasting kind, but it's the first real frisson of *something* I've ever felt."

"And who is the lucky man?" Susan asked.

"Miles' friend."

"Mr Malone?"

"Who? No! Lord Pensby," Edith admitted out loud for the first time.

"But he's so taciturn and reserved! You can't have spent much time in his company."

"I know. Foolish in the extreme, isn't it?" Edith admitted with a bitter laugh. "Miles already suspects I might have some partiality for him and has warned me to look elsewhere for a husband."

"He shouldn't have done that," Susan responded.

"Perhaps not, but he knows Lord Pensby far better than I do," Edith admitted. "But you are my age and also unwed, Susan. Does this mean you also aren't sure if you wish to marry?"

Susan smiled and flushed. "I do want to marry, but I'm not pretty like you, so I'm finding it hard to accept that anyone would want to marry me for anything other than my fortune."

"Susan! What a foolish thing to say! You are extremely fetching, you must know you are," Edith replied hotly.

"You are my best friend and I love you for your defence of me. You know I've been told exactly what I am enough times to realise I have little to offer in the way of looks," Susan responded.

"Who would say such wicked words to you?" Edith asked. "Truly, Susan you are such a lovely package, anyone would be lucky to have you."

"A package?" Susan smiled. "That's a good thing is it?"

"It's a well-known fact that packages always contain the nicer things in life," Edith said authoritatively.

"You are ridiculous," Susan smiled.

"Come. There must be someone we know who is worthy of you," Edith said.

"Don't."

"There is no one you regard?"

"Yes, but it's a hopeless cause," Susan responded.

"Why?"

"The man I'm in love with is hardly aware that I exist, let alone has any interest in me as a wife."

"Then he's a fool!" Edith said hotly.

"That's not a nice way to speak about your brother," Susan said quietly, her tone nervous and unsure.

"Miles? You and Miles? Really? Oh, Susan! You could do so much better than Miles!" Edith exclaimed.

Susan laughed. "Said like a true, loving sister."

"Oh, I don't mean it like that. To see the two people I love the most joined together would be a dream come true, but he is damaged, Susan. The wars he's been involved in…"

"I know. My head tells me it is a futile hope which can only end in making us both miserable, but my heart doesn't listen to my head and continues to hope. Please don't say anything," Susan begged.

"I won't. I feel ashamed that I've never noticed your preference for Miles. It makes me a very poor friend," Edith admitted.

"No. It means my acting skills are finely tuned. I've worked hard to keep everything hidden, but I know my parents are looking for me to marry this season. I'm going to have to let go of my hopes, which are that I will marry the man I want. I'm finding it very hard to cling to the belief my dream would materialise and as a result, I could end by having to accept someone else. The situation both depresses me and terrifies me in equal measure," Susan owned.

"Oh dear, we're both in a pickle, aren't we?" Edith laughed, reaching for her friend's hands and squeezing them gently. "What are we to do?"

"We are going to be open to possibilities," Susan said firmly. "And that includes you getting to know Mr Sage a little more before you decide he's not for you."

"I'll try. I suppose I have to, but I'd much rather spend time with Lord Pensby," Edith said with a sigh.

"No. You have to mean it, Edith. We both have to be really open to potential husbands, or we could end up alone."

"We could always set up an establishment together," Edith suggested hopefully.

"We'd last a week before I threw you out," Susan laughed.

"How rude!" Edith chuckled.

Chapter 8

Ralph rubbed his hand over his face. He was exhausted. A week had passed and he'd hardly had any sleep. His mother had taken a turn for the worse and had required round the clock attention. He could have put most of the burden on the staff, but he refused to, because she was his mother and she needed him. He wasn't bloody-minded enough to refuse help and he worked with the nurse, or her lady's maid. The three of them were the main ones to tend to Lady Pensby, other servants helping to keep the house and gardens as smoothly as possible through a trying time.

The doctor entered the study after knocking on the door. He was beginning to look as haggard as Ralph.

"My lord, I'd like to try something different with your permission," the doctor started.

"What is it?"

"I suggest stopping the laudanum, it clearly isn't having the effect we would wish. I've sent for an alternative treatment to use. It is reported to have had positive results on others with your mother's condition, but it will take a while for it to arrive," the doctor explained.

"Why? We can send someone by express," Ralph said.

"It is coming from the Far East, my lord," came the hesitant response.

"That will take months!"

"I've already taken the liberty of placing the order and expressed the need for it to be sent as fast as is possible. In the meantime, I have something else to offer," the doctor said quickly.

"What?"

The doctor was wary of explaining his next suggestion, but it was all that was left to try outside the asylum treatments. "It was a concoction discovered by Napoleon's troops whilst in Egypt, my lord. I know it sounds far-fetched, but far more eminently qualified men than I have been looking into the effects of it. We need to keep your mother quiet, rested and calm. The less excitable she is, the better. Whilst laudanum just sends her to sleep, this alternative calms the person, but they can still function."

"You make my mother sound as if she's some sort of hysterical female," Ralph said defensively.

"Not at all, my lord. We know it is a calm life the sufferer needs, but even day-to-day life can cause the incidents to occur. This drug seems to reduce that. I think it is worth a try until we receive the herbs I've sent for."

"She is being used as a test case to advance medical science?" Ralph asked.

"Anyone with conditions which are – out of the ordinary, is doing that to some extent, my lord. There are advances in medicine all the time, but some things we still struggle to cure. I'm afraid your mother has one such illness."

"Try your suggestions. At this point there is nothing else we can do," Ralph said bleakly.

The doctor pitied the young man but was glad he'd been given permission to at least try the new drugs. There was little left for them to do without her being admitted to the asylum.

*

Edith stood up from the card table. She smiled at Mr Malone. "You have all my worldly shillings, sir. I shall be reduced to taking in sewing for the remainder of the quarter."

"I shall endeavour to tear every piece of clothing I own to offer recompense," Mr Malone said easily, offering his arm to Edith.

"You have no shame," Edith smiled, accepting a glass of ratafia from a footman.

"None, I'm afraid. I spent too much of my impressionable youth under the charge of your brother."

"I wish you still were. You'd be on guard duty for a month with that comment," Miles said, approaching the pair.

Mr Malone grinned at Miles. "You always were a hard taskmaster. When are you going to give me the offer of your experience at Tattersall's?"

"This week if you like."

"That would be capital. Could I persuade you both to join Charles and myself on a day out to test the animal I decide to buy? Miss King could also join us?" Albert suggested.

"I'm happy to do that. Let's go to Richmond Park. I haven't visited since my return to London," Miles said.

"I'll ask Miss King to accompany us," Edith said, knowing that her friend would need no persuasion to join Miles on a day out.

"Splendid! Charles, our trip is determined to be a success with Lady Edith and Miss King in our company." Mr Malone spoke across two card tables. He received scowls for his impertinence, at which he just grinned.

Later Mr Malone and Mr Sage walked through the streets of London, away from the house where they'd spent the evening and back to their respectable but far more modest accommodation.

"You don't seem to be progressing well with the wealthy Lady Edith," Mr Malone said, all frivolity and charm disappeared. "I can't see any favouritism towards you on her part."

"Yes. She's a cold fish, but her dowry will be worth the wait. She'll come around to my way of thinking. After all, she has little other choice," Mr Sage responded.

"I hope so, because my funds are becoming worryingly low," Mr Malone countered.

"Perhaps you should be mooning around the quiet Miss King?"

"No. She's smitten with Miles. I can see it, but I don't think Miles can. There's no point chasing a no-hoper, although I will be ready to act if Miles should realise she's besotted and rejects the chit."

"He could marry her."

"Miles? Not a chance. He's too clodhopping to notice her. He'll marry a stunning beauty, not a plain squib like Miss King. She's no chance of securing him. But at the moment, you look to be in exactly the same position as the doting Miss King is. Are you sure you aren't chasing a lost cause?"

"No. I tried the quick, more forceful approach and she shied off like a frightened filly. I'm now pursuing the more delicate approach, but I have a plan to bring her around to my way of thinking. She's one who needs to think she knows you through and through. There are ways of convincing her my passion is real. I'm confidant a grand gesture will win her over, because let's face it, there aren't many men flocking around her."

Mr Malone laughed. "Talk like that and you'll have me convinced. It'd better go smoothly though. Miles has got a raging temper and I really don't want to cross him unless I have to."

"Faith, dear Albert, faith. I shall come about, as will Lady Edith."

*

Edith had dismissed her maid when a tap on her bedchamber door interrupted her settling down to read. She wished to be quiet for a while before spending what remained of the morning with her mother. The questions about Miles' friends were getting unbearable. There seemed to be no putting off her parent when she liked someone and felt her daughter should too.

The butler walked into the room, looking kindly, but a little hesitant. "I thought I would bring this directly to you, Lady Edith."

"What is it?" Edith asked, standing and then stopping herself moving forward when she saw a letter on the silver tray.

"It's only just arrived and I thought it prudent to let you see it before her ladyship or my lord had," the butler said gently. The incident with the ripped parcel had been impossible to hide, especially as Lady Longdon had ranted at her daughter for what had felt like hours.

"Oh. I didn't expect to receive any more," Edith said flushing a deep red.

"I thought not. I could always dispose of it..."

"No. I'll deal with it. I probably need to write again, asking for no more to be sent," Edith said, accepting the single letter.

Waiting until the door had been closed behind the butler, Edith sank into the chair nearest the fireplace. She would need to act quickly if either Miles or her mother entered her chamber.

Inside the folded document was another sealed letter. The first one offered an explanation.

Dear Madam,

This letter arrived after the latest instruction from yourself had been received. We perhaps should have destroyed the letter immediately, but we always hope that our 'lonely hearts' find their true match and so have decided to forward it on.

If you wish to respond to the correspondent, we can act as we would have done if we were still running your advertisement.

Wishing you success in your search.

Mr Moorcroft.

Edith let the letter fall onto her lap as she covered her cheeks with her hands. She was mortified. Even the newspaper which ran the advertisements thought they were all desperate women. Miles had been right.

Stinging with shame it was some time before Edith could look at the second letter. Tearing open the wax seal, she spread the paper.

Miss S,

I don't know what I'm hoping to achieve by writing this letter to you. marriage? No. Friendship? Perhaps. All I know is that I don't know what else to do. I need to speak to someone and I'm drawn to you.

If you haven't already burned this, just know that sometimes we all feel as if there is no hope. That those around us just don't understand who we are or what we need. I hope that offers some comfort in your search to find love.

My life is complicated. I am bound my family ties and occasionally the responsibility threatens to overwhelm me. Then I found you and thought you would understand. Perhaps not being able to speak to you in person is the best way, for I don't know how I would put into words what I feel.

It isn't usual for a man to feel fear is it? But I do. Afraid that I am letting down the person who is the most important in my life. How do I overcome that fear? Doctors are struggling to help the person in my care, so what can I offer? It's a hopeless situation which needs me to keep hoping. I don't know how long I can continue without exploding. I am hoping to find relief by putting my thoughts on paper.

I am sorry for the intrusion. Know that I am ashamed of my weakness.

Yours

Mr S

Edith read and reread the letter. It was the strangest piece of correspondence she'd ever received. Even more so when it was supposed to be in response to a romantic advertisement. She was still pondering over it when she was notified that Miss King had come to call.

"Is my mother below stairs?" Edith asked the butler.

"No, m'lady, she remains in her room."

"Please send Miss King to my chamber. We'll have refreshments here," Edith instructed.

"Of course."

Edith walked backwards and forwards across the Axminister rug until her friend was shown into the room.

"Oh, Susan, I'm so glad to see you!" she uttered as soon as her friend walked through the door.

"What's happened? You look all of a flutter," Susan said, quickly taking off her bonnet and going over to Edith.

"I have a confession to make first. I hope you aren't in a hurry," Edith said, sitting with Susan on the chaise longue which she used as a window seat.

"You'd better tell me what's going on," Susan encouraged.

Only pausing when the tray of tea and biscuits were brought in, Edith told her friend about placing the advertisement and the happenings since. She was frank in admitting she'd entered on the scheme which she now considered a foolhardy venture. When she'd finished, she paused to take a sip of tea.

"Do you condemn me for being so foolish?" Edith asked, eventually breaking the silence between the pair.

"No! Although it makes my accusations that you don't really want to be married sound ridiculous if that was the lengths to which you were prepared to go," Susan said.

"Perhaps it was yet another way to keep everyone at arm's length," Edith admitted. "I'm not sure anymore. But this is the strangest of letters." She offered the letter to Susan and waited until it had been read carefully. "Well? What do you think?"

"It's not a love letter, of that we can be certain," Susan answered, musing over what she'd heard and read.

"No. He makes that clear at the start. I would wonder at him writing, except…"

"What?"

"Do you think he knows who he's writing to? It seems as if he's familiar with me. I just have the strangest feeling that he knows me." Edith voiced the terrifying thought for the first time.

"No. How can he?" Susan asked.

"That's what I keep thinking, but the way he writes, it feels as if I should know him," Edith tried to explain.

Susan stared, frowning at the letter, before looking at Edith once more. "Mr S. Do you think it could be Mr Sage?"

"Surely not?" Edith asked in horror. "No. It can't be. How would he have found out that I'd placed the advertisement if even you didn't know? And the tone of it. It's too serious for Mr Sage, he's always carefree and full of laughter."

"He has said he will try and let you see his inner self," Susan pointed out.

"I can't believe he could be so different. If it is him, it is like seeing two completely different people. That would make me more wary of him, not less," Edith said.

"Now don't condemn the poor man for trying," Susan smiled. "Are you going to answer the letter?"

"Maybe."

"You have to. You need to find out who it is."

"I'd rather try and help someone in need. Finding out who he is, is of less importance," Edith admitted.

"I'm as curious as can be," Susan responded. "But I know you're right. He says he doesn't know if he wants a friend, but he certainly sounds like he needs one."

*

Dear Mr S,

I received your letter today and wish to assure you that I am convinced you are not interested in marriage with me.

I didn't burn your letter and felt compelled to write to you in return. I've instructed The Times *that I will accept letters from you. As many as you wish to send and as often as you need to send them.*

I'm not sure if I can be of any help, but I hope by writing you realise you aren't alone. I don't have the same pressures as you do and can only imagine what it must feel like. Is there no outlet for you? Whenever I feel constrained, I admit to riding my horse as hard as the poor beast will let me. There is nothing like feeling the wind trying to knock you off your seat and the risk of stumbling over a rabbit hole to make you feel alive and refreshed when you have survived the experience. I apologise if I sound fickle, but it helps me to remain sane.

I hope your doctor finds something which will ease the suffering of the one you care for so much. I think there are so few people who I truly regard, I would hate to see them suffer. I have experienced loss, and I miss those who are gone every day, but thankfully, they did not suffer as your beloved is. He or she will be in my prayers every night.

Always have hope.

Please know that you are being thought of and wished the very best.

Your friend
Miss S

Chapter 9

Richmond Park spread out before the riders. The green rolled forward as far as the eye could see. The group of horses and riders entered sedately through the gate, but once gathered together in the field, Miles had indicated the direction they should travel and the five horses were spurred into action.

Hooves thundered across the grassland, the whoops of the gentlemen, albeit loud, were lost on the wind. Riders hunkered down over the neck of the horse they were on, to gain that little extra speed over their opponent.

Eventually, the race was won and the group came to a laughing stop. Edith tried to fix her hat as much as possible; she could only imagine the state her hair was in.

"You ride well, Lady Edith," Mr Sage said, turning his horse so he was next to Edith.

"As do you, Mr Sage," Edith said, giving up on her vain attempts to appear more presentable. "Although I wish I was as good as my brother. We were foolish to enter into a race with him. He always wins."

"Hence why Albert refused to have a wager with him," Mr Sage responded, nodding to his friend.

"The next time, I'll have that bet. I just didn't want to push Jester too far on his first real outing with me," Mr Malone said.

"Hah! Excuses, excuses," Miles laughed. "You never could accept being second in anything."

"You didn't mind it when I was willing to take part in any *forlorn hope* which was necessary," Mr Malone responded.

"Yes, volunteering for the attacks which had only a slight chance of success led me to the conclusion that you had a death wish," Miles admitted.

"I did, which was why I was perfect for them."

"I'm glad you lived to tell the tale," Miles said.

"As am I. Now," Mr Malone said. "Enough of these maudlin words. We are here to enjoy the day! Lead on, Miles. Show us this fine park."

They rode until they were exhausted and then stopped on the way back at the first posting house which looked respectable. Hiring a private parlour, the ladies were offered a room to refresh themselves and then joined the gentlemen for some sustenance.

Slicing a chunk of cheese from the thick wedge on the cutting board, Mr Sage turned to Miles. "What other days out can we enjoy in these parts? What's our next adventure to be?"

"I'm afraid our wings are clipped for the next few days at least. In three days it is the party at Curzon Street and mother will be a nightmare from now on with the preparations. She'll need Edith to help out as there's a lot to do apparently," Miles said, with a grin at his sister.

"Don't worry, Miles will be out and about as he always is. He thinks some sort of magic happens when the house is readied for entertainments," Edith responded. "But I shall look forward to seeing you there."

"I hope I can have the first two dances with you," Mr Sage said, before his friend had time to ask.

"Of course," Edith replied.

"And, Miss King, if you would do me the honour?" Mr Malone asked.

"Certainly," Susan replied, but Edith could detect a note of disappointment in her friend's voice.

*

Ralph rested his head on the chair next to his mother's bed. She was sleeping peacefully and for the first time since he'd returned home, it was a more restful, natural sleep.

He'd been beside himself with worry. She'd never been as ill as she had been this time. Now she seemed to be on the mend, he ached with fatigue. Closing his eyes, he sought sleep and although not on the most commodious of seats, he'd discarded his cravat and waistcoat, trying to make himself more comfortable. He thought he would struggle to drop off, but within minutes, he was in a deep slumber.

Waking a while later, he rubbed his hands over his face before realising his mother was watching him. "Hello, dearest," he said. "How are you feeling?"

"Relaxed," Lady Pensby answered. "I don't know what the new medicine is but it soothes and calms me. I feel so much better already."

"It has only been a few days," Ralph cautioned. "You need to take things very slowly."

"I'm not asking to walk through the gardens, just to sit in a chair," came the amused reply.

"I don't want you overtaxing yourself. We can't risk a setback."

"I promise I'll be careful, but I refuse to lie here for the next few years until a spasm finally kills me," Lady Pensby responded. She would have liked her words to sound tart, but unfortunately the drugs made her so serene that she couldn't have sounded anything other than tranquil.

"Don't speak so," Ralph said roughly.

"Oh, my darling boy. I will die one day. It's the natural order of things. The frustration for me is that every time they call you back, it disrupts your efforts to find a bride."

Ralph laughed bitterly. "I don't wish to disappoint you but I'm not trying to find a wife, Mother."

"Now I know you are cross when you stop using my pet name, but don't be. A mother wants to see her children happy. And you aren't at the moment," Lady Pensby soothed.

"I'm just tired. Time with you here will sort that out," Ralph countered. "Don't worry about me."

"I'll always worry about you," Lady Pensby said. "Now when do you return to London?"

"Not for a long time."

"That's not good enough. The season is in full swing. You must return tomorrow."

"A son could get worried about your opinion of him, the way you constantly send me away from you," Ralph teased.

Lady Pensby smiled. "You know full well that I adore you, but I'll dote on you even more when you bring a wife home. Oh, don't worry, you don't need to deny it again. Once you meet a young woman who decides that you are the one, there will be no escape," Lady Pensby said with authority.

"I'm quaking in my boots."

*

Ralph held the two missives in his hand. Two letters from the same house, neither realising the other was being sent.

Miles had sent a letter asking him to attend his mother's soirée if at all possible. He claimed it would help his sanity if there was at least one friend there who he didn't consider a fop or a dandy. Miles' words had brought a smile to Ralph's face. His friend was the most accepting of people, everyone would be given the same genuine welcome. It was a nice gesture, but the reality was that Miles didn't need Ralph to attend at all.

The other, more tempting reason to attend was to see Lady Edith. The feeling of elation he'd felt on receiving her reply had taken him by surprise. Her kind words had touched him deeply. She was the type of person who would help a stranger in need. He had kept the letter in the breast pocket of his waistcoat and it had acted as comfort through the dark days of watching his mother.

He hadn't replied until now and even as he sat at his table in his study, he wasn't quite sure what to write. Staring through the window at the side of the house, he eventually picked up his quill.

A knock on the door disturbed his struggles.

Ralph jumped from his seat when his mother entered the room, on the arms of her lady's maid and a footman. "What the devil—!"

"Language, my dear," Lady Pensby mildly chided. "I wish to speak with you."

"I would have happily come to you," Ralph said, indicating that his mother should be seated in one of the more comfortable chairs near the fireplace. Stoking up the fire, he waited until she was settled. "What is so urgent that you risk a relapse?"

"You do tend to be overly dramatic sometimes," Lady Pensby said with a smile. "I feel weak, but far better than I have in a long time."

Ralph smiled at his mother's insult. "That's good to know. Hopefully when the new drugs arrive, there will be further improvement."

"In the meantime, I have a proposition to make to you."

"Oh?" came the guarded response.

"I'll stay in bed if you return to London," Lady Pensby said, moving her shawl slightly which prevented her from looking into her son's eyes.

"And if I stay?"

"I'll spend as much time as possible below stairs. Every day."

Ralph's eyes narrowed at his mother, who by now was looking at him with the most angelic expression on her face; he could have laughed had he not been frustrated. "You do realise you're blackmailing me?"

"I'd like to think of it as more of a deal for the good of us both."

"I never had you down as a managing mother."

"And I never had you down as a suffocating son."

"A suffocating son?" Ralph asked in disbelief.

Lady Pensby laughed. "I thought that would get your attention. My dear, the more time you spend here, the higher my anxiety increases. It's not good for you to be stuck in a sick room all the time. It isn't the place for a boy."

"You might have noticed I left my boyhood behind some time ago," Ralph said drily.

"More's the pity."

"I'll go to London, but just for one day. I'll attend the Longdon's ball and then return the day after. How does that sound?" Ralph compromised.

"A lot of disruption for one evening," Lady Pensby said. "I'll settle for a week in London."

"I'm sure you would, but I won't. I shall see how I feel after the evening at Longdon's. I might be galloping back to you if it's tedious," Ralph said.

"I hope not. I want you stay for a month, enjoying yourself."

"When I'm away from here, I can't enjoy myself fully," Ralph admitted.

"If that is because you love your home, I applaud you. If it's because of me, I shall box your ears for being foolish," Lady Pensby responded.

Ralph laughed. "Can't it be a bit of both?"

Lady Pensby looked unconvinced.

Chapter 10

Edith saw the letter the moment she entered her bedchamber. There had been no mention of anything arriving by any of the staff, which as Lady Longdon seemed to be everywhere Edith was while the preparations were being undertaken, was a relief as discretion was vital.

She eagerly broke the seal and spread the folded paper. She hadn't been sure he would write back and was so unaccountably glad he had.

Dear Miss S,

You replied to me, which is probably more than I deserve. Thank you for your kind words. I don't want to give you the false impression that I'm some sort of milksop, I'm certainly not, but I have reached a point where I don't know what to do for the best.

Are you ever torn? How do you know you have made the right decision? I'm not sure about any of my decisions recently.

I've been instructed to have some fun by the one I'm so worried about. I'm hardly in the mood for frivolity, but I shall do as I'm bid, for I don't wish to cause any further distress. You have no fear of hearing of my exploits in the morning post, although it would be amusing to cause a stir instead of keeping myself very much in the background.

I hope you are enjoying the season. Are you inundated with letters from your advertisement? I'm quite jealous of the men who can speak with flowery words and flatter a young lady until she is besotted. I'd more than likely receive a scold if I tried to flirt with anyone. Better not to try than to cause offence, don't you think?

You, Miss S, are a beacon of light, I hope you appreciate that you are very special.

Yours
Mr S

Edith read and reread the letter. It was a such a complex document to read, she could hardly make anything of it. He didn't wish to flirt, yet some of his words were certainly flirtatious.

He was obviously a complicated man and she was very much drawn to him. She shouldn't be, but there was something in his words which touched her deeply. She wished she could meet him to reassure that whatever his sufferings, he was not alone.

Placing the letter in the one locked drawer she had, she turned away reluctantly. She wanted nothing but to sit and write back immediately, but there were things to do. The ball was happening the very next day and her mother was becoming more demanding.

Grudgingly, she changed from a practical cotton gown she'd been wearing while sorting out the flowers, into a more respectable morning gown, ready for the visitors who would be calling.

Walking down the stairs, she heard voices in the morning room and hurried to meet the first callers. She hadn't expected anyone to arrive so early and knew that Lady Longdon was still above stairs.

Entering the large square room, Edith faltered slightly before smiling widely and entering with her arms outstretched in greeting.

"My lord! How good it is to see you! Does this mean you are to join us tomorrow evening?" Edith asked, reaching

Ralph and her brother who were standing before the fireplace, chatting amiably.

Ralph reached out automatically before realising the impropriety of greeting Edith in such a familiar way. It would be an insult to her if he were to withdraw his own hands, which were now clasping hers. "Lady Edith, it's a pleasure to see you. Yes, I am attending. Miles tells me it is to be the highlight of the season."

By bringing Miles into the conversation, Ralph was able to step back, therefore releasing Edith's hands to include the three of them. He'd noticed the look of curiosity which Miles had sent in his direction but brazened it out.

"Mama would have it so, but I don't think we can compete with the balls held by the likes of the Duke of Richmond. Now *they* are the highlights of the season," Edith said easily. "You've been away for a while and you are looking pale, my lord. You're not ailing for something are you? We wouldn't wish to force you into spending time with us when you should be resting."

For the first time in his life, Ralph blushed a little. "Thank you for your concern, but I'm fine. Truly."

"That's good to know," Edith said. "There have been some rides out in which your horsemanship was missed."

"Your brother didn't come up to scratch?" Ralph asked.

"Do you really need to ask that?"

"I'll have you know, my counsel has only recently been sought about buying the best horseflesh," Miles interjected.

"I'm afraid it's true. Mr Malone knows my brother of old and insisted on him accompanying him to Tattersall's."

"Malone? Do I know him?" Ralph asked.

"No. We served together. He has an uncle who purchased his commission. He remained abroad after the defeat of Napoleon with his friend, a Charles Sage, although he didn't serve. I don't quite know what he did to be honest. They're both now fully enjoying the season," Miles answered.

"Ah. I see," Ralph said a tad stiffly.

"Would you like me to ring for some refreshments? I hope you will stay a while," Edith said.

"I'm going to save Ralph from being cornered by some of mother's cronies and retire to the study. I'm sure you can deal with them admirably, Edith!" Miles smiled.

"Oh."

"Your brother is a brute, Lady Edith. Could I compensate for his atrocious mistreatment of you by securing the first two dances tomorrow?" Ralph asked, compelled to act once he had witnessed Edith's face drop when hearing they were to leave her.

"I'm already taken for the first two, but I'd be delighted to dance the next two with you," Edith said quickly.

"Of course, it will be my pleasure," Ralph said bowing.

The two gentlemen left Edith to await Lady Longdon and her friends and entered into the masculine sanctuary which was Miles' study. After pouring them both a glass of brandy, Miles smiled. "This is better than copious amounts of tea out of cups which make one feel the giant, they are so tiny. Added to that the delicate cakes which I could eat about a dozen of on my own, Edith is welcome to morning visits."

"You have absolutely no compunction about leaving your sister to deal with everything you find irksome, do you?"

"None at all. And I'll do exactly the same when I get a wife," Miles grinned. "There have to be some advantages to having a sister, or to being leg-shackled."

"You're incorrigible. You really are." Ralph shook his head, grinning. "Which out and outer has beaten me to the first two dances with your sister?"

"You couldn't consider him a top of the tree but he certainly has the looks and address that has endeared him to most of the females within ten miles of here," Miles said, swirling his remaining drink.

"Ah, so Lady Edith has a beau, without the need for the letters," Ralph said.

"He's certainly interested in her. A blind man could see his preference, but as for her feelings on the matter. I honestly don't know," Miles admitted.

"Has he spoken to you?"

"No. Which makes me wonder if she's let him know that she isn't interested. If that's the case though, he must be trying to change her mind," Miles said. "He's very attentive and there are dozens of other ladies who would welcome such a marked preference from him."

"Yes, but do they have everything your sister has? Beauty, charm and money. It's a heady combination."

Miles looked at his friend as if undecided as what to say. "Edith would be the first to say that she wasn't beautiful. Is there something you should be telling me? Or even asking me?"

"What? No! She'd likely murder me in a se'nnight," Ralph blustered.

"As you wish," Miles said, offering Ralph another drink. He didn't fail to notice the gulp of liquid Ralph took once his glass was refilled.

*

Ralph eyed the letter with disgust. He'd returned from Curzon Street to his own lodgings almost storming along the streets. She was encouraging another while writing to him. He'd never felt jealousy in his life and he didn't know what to do with the rage burning in his gut.

Walking up and down his drawing room offered no relief while the letter mocked him from the silver platter containing his post.

Eventually, he tore at the seal, ripping the corner of the page in his anger. The damage was enough to calm him instantly. "She owes me nothing," he muttered to himself before starting to read.

Dear Mr S,

I understand you completely when you say you are torn! I would love to be in the countryside right now. Spending my days out of doors as much as possible. Instead I am confined to the drawing rooms across London and I'm so bored I could scream.

Thankfully, I have a brother who indulges me with long horse rides which affords a little escape. Unfortunately, it is not enough. I will the season to be at an end and then I can truly plan for my future. An occurrence in which I will be able to plan my own destiny. Not easy when I have a mother who is desperate for me to marry anyone who asks. I know things would be different if my father were here, but he isn't, so there is no point longing to speak to him. Wishing for the impossible achieves nothing.

Sending in the advertisement has been productive in two ways. It has helped me to see what I really want, something I wasn't sure of before. Secondly, it's introduced me to you. My mysterious friend, who offers me an outlet for my deepest feelings. I hope I offer you the same – a safe place to speak your mind. I've told you more than I should. Perhaps, even now you know who I am. I had to explain myself fully to show you I understand some of your worries and troubles. I hope it helps.

One last point I wish to raise. You claim that you aren't one for flowery speeches, but your words are dear to me.

Your friend
Miss S

Ralph sat back. He'd been riddled with jealousy, but her words had soothed him. He was a cad for taking advantage of her, knowing who she was meant her words gave him an insight he wouldn't have normally, but he was adrift and she was his anchor. Even if she didn't realise it.

He would reveal himself to her. Just not quite yet.

Chapter 11

Edith had commissioned a new dress. It was frivolous and shallow but she wanted to look her best. She had hoped he would attend and now she would spend an hour or more in his company. She had missed him.

Opening the drawer, she took out the last letter she'd received from her mystery writer. "Why can't you be one and the same?" she whispered to the ink on the page. Sighing, she placed the letter back in its secure home and hid the key. Catching her reflection in the looking glass she grimaced.

"There's no point wishing for the impossible. One is handsome, rich, abrupt in manner, yet I'm drawn to him. The other could be poor, ugly, but has a way with words and a vulnerability which tugs at my heart. I've just got to enjoy my time with Lord Pensby tonight, for I don't know when I'll see him again."

Leaving her bedchamber, she met her mother at the top of the staircase.

"You are looking charming tonight, Edith. I expect there will be at least one proposal by tomorrow if what I hope will happen comes to fruition," Lady Longdon said with a nod of approval at her daughter's attire.

Edith sagged a little at her mother's words. One thing which had become clear in the preceding days was that Lady Longdon favoured Mr Sage and Edith did not.

Miles was waiting at the bottom of the stairs and after making a fuss of his mother, he twirled Edith around. "You are looking delightful, Edith. That colour really suits you."

Edith had chosen a pale blue silk gown, with puff sleeves and delicate white lacing along the edges. The bottom of the skirt was decorated with white and blue ribbon gathered in scalloped edges. The skirt billowed out slightly as she spun, a lovely effect to occur when one was dancing. She had agreed to wear an aquamarine and diamond necklace from the family jewels. The whole effect brought out the faint blue hue in her otherwise grey eyes.

Not one to wear powders and beauty patches as her mother and others of the older generation were inclined to do, Edith just wore black on her lashes and red lip colour. Her flush of anticipation gave her cheeks a heightened colour and sparkling eyes, which added to her overall good looks.

"I hope tonight is a success," Lady Longdon said, before the doors were opened to welcome the first guests.

"Of course it will be, Mother," Miles responded easily. "Our parties are known to offer each guest as much food and drink as they could possibly wish for. What else does one need to guarantee a good night?"

Edith laughed. "You are a rascal, Miles."

"But lovely with it," Miles answered before turning to greet his guests.

*

It was the second dance before Mr Sage started to hint once more of what he wished to happen. He was not put off by Edith's gentle redirecting of his unsubtle words.

Eventually, he seemed to give up all pretence of subtlety and suggestion.

"Lady Edith, please allow me to speak to your brother," Mr Sage said as they stood at the bottom of the set.

"I'd rather you didn't," Edith responded, flushing.

"But I thought…" Mr Sage ground his teeth. "The words we have shared about our inner feelings. I thought we understood each other more so than most people who are acquainted. I know I shouldn't presume, but when I've confessed my inner turmoil, I thought you understood."

Edith faltered. "Your inner turmoil?"

"Yes, I've shared things with you that I haven't told another soul. I thought we had a connection beyond that of mere acquaintances," Mr Sage continued.

Wiping her hand across her brow, Edith frowned. "Do you mean – is it you?"

"Is who me?"

"I'm very confused how you found out it was I," Edith continued, her emotions agitated.

"It was easy to find the one I was drawn to more than anyone else in my past, present or future," Mr Sage said. "I do think it's time I spoke to your brother and made our feelings official."

"I'm sorry, Mr Sage. I feel a little unwell. Please don't say anything to Miles just yet. I need to think," Edith said, faltering a little.

"Of course, Lady Edith. Allow me to escort you to a seat. Shall I bring you some negus?" Mr Sage offered.

"Yes, please. That would be kind. Thank you," Edith answered, feeling quite lightheaded.

As she sat, Susan approached her friend. "Edith, are you ill? I saw you leave the dance and immediately withdrew myself. Mr Malone has gone to seek out Mr Sage."

"Oh, Susan! I've had it all wrong!" Edith wailed. "I wanted it to be Lord Pensby, but it isn't, it's Mr Sage!"

Susan immediately sat down next to Edith. "The letters? Are you sure?"

"He all but admitted it just then. He wants to speak to Miles and even though he's the one who wrote the letters, I can't, Susan, I can't marry him!"

"Edith, shh. Gather yourself. Someone will notice something is amiss," Susan chided gently.

"I'm sorry. My head is in such a swirl. How can I have made such a mistake? I thought the man who wrote the letters knew me, but for it to be him – no!"

"You liked the man who wrote the letters, Edith. Perhaps you aren't seeing Mr Sage for who he truly is?"

"Surely, surely, there can't be such a difference between what he writes and how he is. He's flighty and a rascal, I'm sure of it," Edith whispered, as she saw the return of the two gentlemen, both carrying glasses.

"Ladies, we brought double supplies," Mr Malone said handing both a glass. "It's a real crush everywhere, so we thought it prudent to bring more than one glass, as you might need more."

"That's very kind of you," Susan replied. "I'm sure Lady Edith will feel more the thing soon."

"The dance is ending," Edith said. "Please don't let me detain you from your next partners."

"Don't worry about that," Mr Sage said, showing no inclination to leave Edith's side.

Edith looked at Susan with an unspoken appeal and her friend sprang into action.

"Mr Sage, I do believe we are promised for the next. I'm sure Lady Edith will appreciate our absence. She is quite well, just needing a moment to gather herself," Susan chivvied and bullied the two gentlemen so they moved away from Edith.

Edith wasn't alone for long, as Ralph approached her.

"There you are! I thought you were reneging on our dances," he said with a smile. Noticing Edith's pale complexion his demeanour changed immediately. "Are you unwell, Lady Edith?"

"I've just received a shock. It is nothing really, but I do wish I could swap this glass of negus for a glass of brandy," Edith said with a sigh.

Ralph laughed. "You never cease to surprise me, Lady Edith. Come, I know your brother has some excellent brandy in his study. We shall make our escape."

"I shouldn't," Edith faltered. Going into a private room with a single man was a sure way of creating even more trouble than she was already in.

"I'll get your brother," Ralph said, understanding her reluctance.

"Thank you."

Miles came across to Edith, who had removed herself to the hallway. One or two persons were milling about but apart from a nod in their direction, Edith had managed to escape entering into conversation with anyone.

"What's amiss?" he asked.

"I've been foolish. Again. And I need a drink to fortify myself. If any of this reaches my mother, I shall need a decanter," Edith responded dully.

The two men exchanged a glance, but Miles led the way into his study. "We can't remain here for long," Miles cautioned.

Edith had seated herself in front of the fire and stared unseeingly into the flames. Accepting the glass of brandy from Miles, she swallowed it in one gulp. Letting out a slight shudder, she turned to give Miles her now empty glass.

"What?" Edith asked, looking at the two astounded expressions looking at her. "I needed that."

"You drank it without a splutter," Miles pointed out.

"Yes. You don't think I could get through three years of being in mourning and caring for mother without the occasional glass of brandy, do you? Times were hard," Edith answered with a shrug.

Miles looked dumbstruck, but Ralph started to laugh. "Lady Edith, the gamester and hardened drinker," he chuckled.

Despite the feeling of desolation in her stomach, Edith smiled. "Now you have seen all my vices, my lord."

"Gamester?" Miles asked.

"It's a long story, brother. Unfortunately, there are more pressing matters to discuss," Edith said.

"I should leave you," Ralph offered quickly.

"This will only take a moment," Edith said, standing and brushing down her dress. She felt emboldened with the brandy coursing through her veins. "Miles, do not under any circumstances give your agreement to Mr Sage's proposal. If you see him near mother, please interrupt them, for I'm sure he will try and gain her support. I don't care what you have to do, but do not give him any hope that he will ever receive my hand in marriage."

"Edith, you are of age. He knows he doesn't need my permission," Miles pointed out.

"I can't marry him, Miles. Lord Pensby, are you well?" Edith had noticed Ralph had changed colour. He looked like he might actually faint.

Ralph turned to Miles, his expression dark. "Let me throw him out."

Miles blinked. He'd never seen his friend look so ill and then forbidding within the same moment, but it only took him a second to respond. "No. I refuse to let my mother's party be spoiled in such a way. The man has done nothing wrong. There's no crime in asking someone to marry them."

He turned to Edith. She seemed as struck by Ralph's expression as he had, but she forced herself to turn to her brother. "He said some things – nothing bad, but I'm confused. All I know for sure is if he's the one who's written those words, I've been completely mistaken."

"I have no idea to what your referring to, Edith. I think the brandy has gone to your head. I accept you don't wish to marry him, so for goodness sake, don't let yourself be alone with him. If you refuse him, he could try to compromise you."

"She won't be alone for a moment," Ralph ground out.

"Thank you," Edith responded. Ralph's appearance of jealousy, or was it just support of his best friend, confused Edith even more. She forced down the feelings of wretchedness which would no doubt overwhelm her when the evening had ended. Until then she would paste a smile on her face and continue.

Crossing over to the decanter, she filled her glass and took another glug of liquid. "Come," she said, setting her shoulders. "Let's get through this evening."

Ralph held out his arm. "We still have one dance. No one will approach you while you are in my company."

"Thank you. I know I will be protected if I'm with you," Edith responded.

"Always," Ralph responded.

"I wish you had sent them. I so wanted it to have been you," Edith said quietly. There was no acknowledgement that Ralph had heard her as they returned to the ballroom.

Edith tried to place a smile on her face, but it probably looked as false as it felt. For the first few minutes they danced in silence, but eventually Ralph broke the strained atmosphere.

"It's to your credit that you're prepared to stand up for what you truly want," he said gently.

Edith grimaced. "Most people would class me as a fool."

"Thankfully, I don't consider myself one of the masses."

"No. You don't give a fig what anyone thinks, do you?"

Ralph paused. "I do. Yes."

"Really? You don't act as if you do," Edith responded, her interest piqued.

"Trust me. I do. Which is why I admire your ability to say no."

"I might not feel so steadfast when my mother has torn a strip off me," Edith replied with a ghost of a smile.

"Your brother will support you."

"He does. I detest setting him against mother, but I can't agree to something I object to so strongly," Edith admitted.

Ralph seemed to consider his next words carefully. "Lady Edith, believe me when I say, I wish things could be different. That I long to be able to offer you protection of my own, but I cannot."

Edith frowned. "I'm not sure I understand your meaning, my lord."

"Would it sound ridiculous if I said, neither do I?" Ralph laughed, self-mockingly. "I just know I wish there was more I could offer."

*

Lady Longdon berated her daughter for a full two hours after the last guest had departed. Even her son could not distract her from her mission of browbeating her daughter into accepting a proposal from a handsome man.

"But I don't love him!" Edith eventually said, after trying time and again to convince her mother that she was justified in refusing Mr Sage.

"Fustian! He's a charming, handsome gentleman! What else could a girl like you wish for?" Lady Longdon responded cuttingly.

"A girl like me?" Edith asked, her eyes glinting.

"Edith…" Miles cautioned.

"No. Let Mother speak. She obviously has a view of me that I think I should hear," Edith said.

"You go around, thinking you're above the company we are in, and yet you remain nothing but a wallflower," Lady Longdon responded. "How many dances have you sat out over the season? How many men send you flowers, visit this house, trying to vie for your attention? None. It's been laughable watching you look down your nose at the poor souls who have foolishly tried to be nice to you. And now look at you! Refusing the only decent man you are ever likely to meet! You are a fool, Edith, and I want no more to do with you."

"Mother, there is no need for this. What you say is wrong and unfair," Miles said, his tone sharper than normal when speaking to his parent.

"No, it isn't. You haven't been here for the last few years, watching your sister become insufferable as she acted the lady of the house." Lady Longdon responded without the slightest remorse at being taken to task by her son.

"I was dealing with the deaths of my father and two brothers!" Edith defended herself. "You were unable to do anything, so I took the burden from you. I thought I was helping."

"I had lost my sons and my husband; of course I was prostrate with grief. I didn't expect you to run roughshod over everything in the process. I only came to London to get you off my hands finally. And now, it looks like you're even interfering in that plan!"

Tears welled in Edith's eyes. Never before had she been spoken to in such a manner. She saw Miles was fit to explode at their mother, but she raised her hand slightly to stop him. Standing, she looked at her brother, whose eyes held nothing but sympathy. His expression nearly undid her, but she managed to swallow the lump in her throat.

"Miles, please arrange for me to return home the day after tomorrow. I would like the opportunity to take my leave of a few friends, which I will do in the morning. I will be ready to leave first thing on Saturday," Edith said, moving to the door.

"Don't expect me to come with you," Lady Longdon threw over her shoulder.

"I wouldn't, Mother," Edith responded, formally addressing her parent. "In fact, it is my intention to have left Barrowfoot House by the time you return. Miles, I will be seeking the advice of our solicitor about setting up my own establishment. If you could ask him to visit me once I return to Barrowfoot, I would be grateful."

"Edith, there really isn't the need—"

"There is every need, Miles. How are we to recover from the words which have been uttered? Far too much has been said," Edith responded. "I'll bid you goodnight."

When the door had closed behind Edith, Miles turned on his mother. "Mama, you are a fool! You will regret this day for a long time to come. Who is going to pander to you in the way Edith has done? Who will do your bidding without question? If you think I am to be the drudge Edith has been, you are to be sadly mistaken," he scolded. "I might not be in the frame of mind to marry, but if you think I have the urge to spend my time following you around like some sort of lapdog, you have misunderstood my intentions of returning home. I came home for peace, not to be at your beck and call!"

Miles had never spoken to his mother so harshly and she looked stunned for a few moments. It wasn't long though before she reverted to type and started to cry and remonstrate her son for being a poor being in mistreating his only living parent.

Walking out of the drawing room in disgust, Miles indicated to the butler. "Send my mother's maid to her, and warn her she'll have a darned long night. I shall arrange for suitable recompense to be added to her wages. She will earn it over the coming weeks. If my mother puts extra strain on any other member of staff, let me know and I will show my appreciation of their tolerance," Miles instructed.

"Yes, m'lud," the butler replied, without showing a flicker of surprise at the words. He'd cleared everyone out of the vicinity of the drawing room when it was apparent Lady Longdon was in one of her moods. He would not allow servants to talk about their employers and Lady Longdon very often gave a poor impression of herself.

Moving away from his master, he noticed with regret the grim expression on Miles' face as he started to climb the stairs. The poor young man had been through enough and in some respects was still suffering, he didn't need the angst his mother would now inflict on her family. He was burdened enough.

*

Edith ignored the scratch on the door and groaned when it opened and Miles appeared, a tentative smile on his face. "I can't apologise," Edith said, blowing her nose and drying her eyes. "Please don't ask me to."

"I would never expect that of you," Miles said, walking across to his sister and enfolding her in an embrace. "How often has she had explosions like that?"

"Too many to remember every one," Edith admitted, resting her head on her brother's shoulder. "This one was particularly spectacular though."

"I've torn a strip off her," Miles admitted. "She crumbled and is currently wailing downstairs."

"Oh, dear Lord!" Edith responded. "She'll never forgive me for turning you against her. It's a good thing I'll be setting up my own home."

"Don't leave, Edith," Miles said.

Edith pulled away from her brother and sat down near her dressing table. "I have to. You know I was longing to return home anyway and tonight has just made that wish even more prominent. I can't stay here, Miles."

"There are more men than Sage," Miles cajoled.

"It's not really about him," Edith admitted. "He's just the one who has unintentionally brought everything to a head. I can't be with Mother. She will give me no support and I can't bear to have a rift in the family which would be open to public scrutiny. She won't think twice of telling anyone and everyone how I've wronged her. I wouldn't mind if I was as poor as a church mouse and desperate for someone to provide for me. With what I would bring to a marriage, it shouldn't be that hard to find someone decent."

"I want to see you settled, just as much as she does," Miles admitted.

"But you would not force me into a marriage I didn't want."

"No," Miles acceded. "I don't want you setting up home on your own though. That's a step too far."

"I'm going to think about my options when I return home. I promise I won't rush into anything, but I will consider which of our wider family would be suitable in being a companion for me. For I will have to set up an establishment at some point," Edith said.

"Who would you ask?"

"I don't know. Perhaps Mildred," Edith said, but started to smile at her brother's horrified expression.

"Isn't she about ninety and half blind?" he asked.

"A perfect companion for me then," Edith said. "She won't know what I'm doing, but I'll still be considered respectable with her living with me."

"You, my dear, are doing nothing without my agreement. You might be of age, but you are completely outrageous and can't be trusted," Miles said tartly.

Edith laughed. "You brute. I knew I wouldn't get away with my wild plans to set up my own gaming hell."

Miles smiled, but it was tinged with sadness. "I'm sorry you had to wait so long for your come out. Things could have been so different if it had happened sooner."

Edith became serious and walking to wrap her arms around her brother, she kissed his cheek. "It doesn't matter. I have you and my friends. I shall prepare to be an aunt to as many children as you and your future wife produce and encourage them all to get into all kinds of mischief. I'll be an honorary aunt to Susan's children when she settles down, so my life will be full of little ones. I'll make sure they are all wild."

"That, my sweet, I can believe and the thought of it terrifies me," Miles said, giving Edith a warm embrace before leaving her in peace. They both would get little sleep in what remained of the night.

Chapter 12

Edith walked downstairs late in the morning. She'd requested breakfast in her room and had been told that her mother hadn't left her bed as she was feeling unwell. Edith would have normally been forced to endure her mother's chamber for the rest of the day while she tended to her every whim. Today was different. As she was leaving London the following morning, she felt no guilt at leaving her mother to her maid.

When she reached the bottom of the stairs, the butler brought a silver tray over to her. "A letter, Lady Edith," he said quietly.

Edith hadn't expected to receive any more letters, so took it reluctantly. Opening it while she stood in the hallway, her stomach fluttered when she read the words.

Dear Miss S,

You looked beautiful last night. You don't seem to appreciate the effect you have on those around you. I wish you did, although your modesty does you credit.

There. I have revealed something of myself, I am one in your company, but don't fear, I would never betray you, or harm you or your reputation. My regard is too high for that.

I'm not a man who sends flowers, but believe me when I say, you were most appealing in every sense. There was no one else present who could compete with you in my eyes.

Yours, with admiration,
Mr S

Edith had paled a little at reading the words. He knew who she was. Could it be Mr Sage? She was clinging to the fact that it couldn't be, surely he would have mentioned something about what they'd exchanged last night. It could mean that if he did try and seek an audience with her brother and was turned down, he could reveal her secret. She would be the laughing stock of society. She sighed, it was a good thing that she was leaving town.

Placing her bonnet on her head, she smiled through the looking glass when she spied Miles walking out of his study.

"Nice to see you up and about," she said pleasantly, ignoring the fact that they both had dark circles under their eyes, hinting at the rough night both had endured.

"Couldn't sleep," Miles admitted.

"Me neither," Edith responded. "But I am going to visit Susan and say my goodbyes. Is there anything you need whilst I am out?"

"No. Are you going alone?"

"As she lives exactly ten houses away, there is no need to be accompanied. I was trying to decide whether or not to go shopping, but I can't honestly face it. Spending the afternoon with Susan will be perfect and I don't need to be escorted for that," Edith responded.

"In that case, I shall see you tonight. I expect it will be just the two of us dining. I doubt Mother will be ready to face either of us," Miles said, kissing Edith's cheek.

They said their goodbyes and Edith left the house. She took a lungful of the smoke-filled air and was thankful she would only be spending one more day in the capital. She longed for the wide-open spaces and fresh, crisp air of her home.

She soon reached the abode of her friend and was greeted with pleasure. When Edith had explained what had gone on after the ball and the result of the argument, Susan sat back in her seat.

"It saddens me to hear that the situation with your mother has deteriorated to such an extent. It was clear she favoured Mr Sage from almost the moment he was introduced to us," Susan said.

"My folly was to not realise earlier how much I objected to the thought of being married to him. I should have been more forceful against his prior hints and protestations of regard. I can't lay all the blame at his door for his continued attentions," Edith acknowledged.

"Anyone with half a brain would have seen that you had no real interest in him. You were friendly, but not encouraging," Susan defended her friend.

"I suppose he might have thought me coy. There are many who would be. He wasn't to know I would never embark on such scheming behaviour," Edith said. "Added to that, I've no idea what my mother was saying to him, but it was almost certainly encouragement. I'm just glad there can be no doubt of my feelings, or lack of them now."

"I'll be sorry to see you go. The season won't be the same without you here," Susan admitted.

"I can't stay any longer, Susan, but after the season, whether you are married, or not, you must come to visit me."

"I won't be married, not unless my parents carry out their threat of choosing a husband for me," Susan responded dully.

"I would love to have you as my sister, but I don't think Miles is ready to wed. He's hinted at being damaged. I think there is a lot going on with him that we don't realise. I doubt he would admit to anything if I tried to probe, he's too proud to acknowledge he's suffering," Edith said.

"I know and I don't expect anything from him in reality. You know what it's like to long for someone but know it's fruitless. I accept he isn't interested in me, beyond being your friend, he's probably hardly noticed me," Susan replied.

"In that regard he's a fool," Edith smiled.

"Thank you for your unwavering support! Have you thought what you are going to do about the letters?"

"Oh, I have some news with regards to that," Edith said, pulling the latest letter out of her reticule. "I admit to being a little concerned that whoever is writing to me, knows who I am."

"Yes. I would be, but it doesn't sound like it's Mr Sage. Surely he wouldn't be so complimentary after last night?" Susan reasoned.

"It's all very confusing," Edith admitted. "But I must take the next step into my own hands and write to Mr Sage and ask him not to send any more letters. I feel very confused that I could feel a connection with his words, but not with him in person. It feels all wrong somehow that I just can't put the two people together. Yet his hints would suggest it's him and makes me mistrust the written word even more," Edith admitted.

"It's all very strange," Susan agreed.

"I shall take my leave of you, Susan. It's time I was returning to ensure everything I want is packed and ready to depart early tomorrow. There's no point in delaying further," Edith said, standing.

Susan also stood and the two friends embraced, promising to write and professing their regard for each other.

Edith left the house with mixed feelings. She wished Miles could see Susan as something other than his sister's friend, but she didn't hold out any hope. There was no point in trying to interfere, Miles had a wall around him since his return. While Edith understood the reason it was there, she had no idea on how to go about breaching it. To try would to alienate her brother and she couldn't risk that. Not even for Susan.

Turning back towards her own house, she became aware that a landau and four had stopped at the side of the pavement on which she walked. The hood which covered the seats facing forward was hiding the occupants, but the other side was down.

Edith stifled a groan when Mr Sage sat forward in his seat and opened the door himself, even though a footman sat at the rear of the vehicle.

"Lady Edith, I'm so glad to have seen you. I was on my way to pay a call at your address," Mr Sage said, jumping nimbly onto the pavement in front of Edith.

"My mother isn't seeing visitors today, sir. She's a little tired after the exertions of last night."

"It was you I wished to have a word with. Could I trouble you to take a drive around Hyde Park with me? I would appreciate some time with you in which I can speak plainly without being overheard."

"I don't think—" Edith started.

"I assure you, I shall not inflict any unwanted attentions. It's purely just to try to explain myself and to ensure we part as friends."

"We do part as friends," Edith insisted.

"Please. Indulge me in this," Mr Sage appealed, his smile lighting up his eyes.

"I must return home soon," Edith said, capitulating to the request.

"Just a little time and we shall understand each other perfectly," Mr Sage said, pulling the step of the landau down and helping Edith into the carriage.

As soon as he closed the door, the carriage moved off. Mr Sage seated himself next to Edith and turned to her. "I'm so glad you agreed. I was mortified the way last night turned out. I had hoped to be announcing our engagement today."

"I'm sorry. I do like you and have enjoyed your company but I could never agree to a marriage with you. I should have been clearer about my feelings from the start," Edith acknowledged.

"Perhaps, but I fixed my interest with you as soon as I saw you and I don't easily get deterred."

"Mr Sage, why are we turning left onto Half Moon Street?" Edith asked, looking at her surroundings with some concern.

"I've instructed my man to enter the park on the south carriage drive. Nothing to worry about," Mr Sage said easily.

Edith had stiffened and remained seated bolt upright. She didn't feel at all comfortable. She'd never trusted him completely and, feeling vulnerable, she was on her guard. "Mr Sage, I'm sorry about not being more forthcoming in my wishes, but we would never suit."

"That is where our opinions differ, I'm afraid, Lady Edith," Mr Sage responded. "And in this case, I'm afraid that my wishes will have to outweigh yours."

"I don't understand," Edith said.

"I favour you above anyone else in society. I have to be honest and admit that your fortune is the main attraction, but as you come as part of a package, I'm sure we'll rub along splendidly."

"Sir, I have told you we won't be marrying. Please stop the carriage and allow me to alight. There can be nothing gained from prolonging this conversation," Edith demanded in her coldest tone.

"I'm sorry to disappoint you, Lady Edith, but I'm unable to indulge you in your request," Mr Sage said with a smile, which wasn't quite as cherubic as previous ones had been. "I've been looking for someone like you and I've invested too much time and money for my efforts to be wasted. We are on our way to the docks, where we will board a boat. There will be no dash to the border for us, we're going to sail around the coast to Scotland."

"You are preposterous, sir!" Edith exclaimed. "Do you think I will comply with your scheme. Why, I have only to shout to passers-by now and your scheme will be foiled."

"I don't think you should. For you'll only be ruined, when I grab and kiss you for everyone to see and the result will be marriage to me because of your actions. If you wish a wedding surrounded by gossip, go ahead, shout and scream all you wish. A pity your mother would be made seriously ill by the scandal, her being of a delicate nature," Mr Sage said with a nonchalant shrug. "Better that we sort everything out in a quieter, more refined way."

Edith was furious. He'd clearly thought everything out. They were bowling along at a fast pace, far too fast for her to be able to jump out of the carriage without sustaining serious injury, or worse. She couldn't shout out; it would be mortifying and a guaranteed way of ruining herself in the process as he'd already pointed out.

Come, Edith, think, she cursed inwardly. There must be a way out of this. You can't be kidnapped in an open carriage for goodness sake. She would not accept her situation was irredeemable, but she had to think quickly, there was limited time to act.

As the carriage turned left down Piccadilly and closer to the Thames, she had to have something answered. Turning blazing eyes on her captor she looked at him with disgust.

"How could you be so different? How could you write those words and yet act in such a dastardly way? It doesn't make any sense, but I need to know," she asked.

"I have no idea to what you refer," Mr Sage answered, looking genuinely confused.

"The letters. You wrote such revealing words, expressed such emotions," Edith said.

"What letters? I haven't written any letters to anyone," Mr Sage responded.

"You don't know about the advertisement?" Edith asked, her heart starting to lift a little.

"Are you crazed? You truly are speaking nonsense," Mr Sage responded roughly. "I think it's time you learned that I like a quiet wife and stop your ramblings. Be silent, woman."

Edith turned away from him and laughed with relief. It wasn't him. She hadn't been going mad when thinking that there were two men involved. There *were*. He wasn't the one writing to her! She could have almost hugged him if it hadn't been that there literally were no redeeming features to him, apart from his looks and she'd never really cared for those.

The revelation had made Edith certain about one thing, she wasn't going to be forced into marriage to this fortune hunter, whatever the cost.

As the carriage approached the junction of Piccadilly and St James's Street, the vehicular traffic increased and the landau was forced to slow. The driver cursed loudly at whoever was blocking their way. It was clear he was very keen to keep the speed of the horses at a brisk pace, to prevent her trying to escape.

Edith watched carefully without making it obvious. She would only get one chance and she couldn't let it fail. If she could get out of the carriage, she presumed that Mr Sage wouldn't risk making a scene. Being inside a carriage with a gentleman carried some risk, which Mr Sage had depended on. She'd climbed into the carriage willingly, which would be reported by her captor. If she managed to get onto the pavement though and efforts were made to drag her into the vehicle, it would more likely look like a kidnapping. That wouldn't be received well by anyone who observed the action. She couldn't be condemned for making a noise to prevent her being dragged into a carriage. And she would make noise.

The carriage lurched, Edith gasped, "Miles!" and pointed to the side furthest away from her.

Mr Sage jumped forward to see her brother as, at the same time Edith flung open the door and jumped onto the road.

She stumbled and fell, her gloved hands landing in the dirt of the roadway, her dress trailing through goodness knew what detritus on the ground. Not stopping to check if she'd hurt herself, or brush herself down, she jumped to her feet and hurried from the carriage. She was desperate to try to put some distance between herself and Mr Sage. She shook at the thought that there were three men who could pursue her, if the coachman and footman were called to help. Pushing terror to one side she urged herself to move forward.

Hearing noises behind her, she knew that she was being followed; one of them at least was giving chase. The only people around were giving her a wide berth. She knew she must look a state. Trying to stop herself from running, she concentrated on walking as quickly as she could, her heart pounding loudly in her ears.

Within a few seconds she was grabbed roughly. "Don't be a fool," Mr Sage hissed. "Do you want me to throw you over my shoulder and carry you back to the carriage, or do you want to walk?"

Edith stood firm. "Unhand me, sir!" she said loudly.

Mr Sage glowered at her, but kept a tight grip. "Come, my dear, you are overwrought." He started to pull her towards the coach, digging his fingers into her flesh so hard she cried out in pain.

Edith was no match for Mr Sage but she wasn't going to go meekly back with him. Pulling her gloves off and throwing them to the floor, she wriggled, but it only meant his fingers dug deeper into her flesh. At least the footman and driver had remained on the landau, or there would be no hope for her.

She decided it was time to take further action as no one else seemed to be willing to help her. She flung herself in front of Mr Sage and with all of her strength used her free hand to slap him across the face.

Mr Sage stumbled backwards and instinctively let go of her as his hand went to his face. "You bitch!" he spat, but Edith was already running away from him.

No longer caring what sort of a scene she created, Edith lifted her skirts and ran with all her might. She was covered in dirt, must look like some kind of doxy, or madwoman, but she didn't care. Getting away from her captor was her only aim.

A horseman pulled in at the side of her. She was aware of her name being called, but kept moving. If she stopped, he could grab her again.

"Edith! Stop!" came the commanding voice of her brother, as he slid off his horse and grabbed her in one fluid movement.

Finally recognising the voice of her brother, Edith sagged with relief and collapsed into Miles' arms with a sob. "He was trying to force me to elope with him," she said, whilst clinging to her brother.

"The damned cur!" came a growl from the opposite side of Miles.

Ralph flung his stovepipe hat to the ground and ran after the now retreating Mr Sage. Ralph soon caught up with the smaller man and spun him around. "Only brave near women are you?" he uttered before his fist connected with Mr Sage's chin.

Mr Sage went sprawling to the ground, but Ralph hauled him to his feet. "I'm going to kill you and then if I find out that you hurt her, I'm going to kill you all over again," he said, before landing a second punch.

Edith hid her face in Miles' coat, unable to watch the fight. After a while, Miles shouted to his friend. "Enough, Ralph. He's not worth hanging for."

"Is he not?" Ralph growled back, picking up Mr Sage who seemed barely conscious.

"No." Miles separated himself from his sister. "Wait here," he said gently, standing her next to his horse.

He approached Ralph and the now slumped Mr Sage, whose face was no longer cherubic by any stretch of the imagination. Miles leant down so his face was close to the kidnapper. "I'd advise you to leave London as soon as you can because once I have my sister settled at home, I'm going to come looking for you. My hands are tingling in the expectation of strangling the life out of you and I'd hate to disappoint them. When I've finished with you, I'm then going to find your friend and do the same to him. You've clearly been using my family and I don't take kindly to that. Not. At. All. Do I make myself clear?"

Mr Sage nodded, hardly able to open his eyes, even if he wanted to. The menace in Miles' voice had terrified him more than the brutality of the beating from Ralph.

"Good. Then there is no doubt what you'll be receiving if you are foolish enough to remain in London, or to return during the next ten years. You aren't going to prey on innocents whilst I have breath in my body."

Miles let go off Mr Sage's frock coat collar which he'd been holding him up with and the injured man slumped to the ground. Turning to the servants, he indicated to them. "I hope you are ashamed of yourselves, helping a scoundrel like this. Get him and yourselves out of my sight."

A crowd had gathered to watch such a spectacle. They had been interested once the fight had started, unlike when they had seen Edith fleeing from her captor. Miles stared at those nearest to him with such a forbidding look that they turned away, shamefaced.

When the street began to move in its more natural rhythm, he turned to Edith and Ralph. "We need to get you both cleaned up. Edith, climb up in front of me. It's not ideal, but the quicker we remove ourselves from the street, the better. Ralph you come with us."

"But Mother…" Edith started.

"My house is just around the corner. We should go there," Ralph offered.

"Good idea," Miles said. "Come." He indicated to Edith and lifted her up so she could sit in front of his saddle, her legs dangling to the side. It wasn't ideal, but it would cause fewer stares than if she was walking through the streets as dishevelled as she was.

Ralph gingerly took the reins of his own horse and swung onto the saddle. He winced when closing his fists over the leather of the reins.

"We'd best get some ice on your knuckles if you wish to move them tomorrow," Miles said.

"I think it might be too late," Ralph grimaced. He flicked a look at Edith before turning his horse around and starting in the direction of his home.

Chapter 13

Edith entered Ralph's home with more than a slight interest. She surreptitiously looked around the drawing room into which they were shown. It was stylish, without being too sparse; gentlemen were usually prone to keep furnishings to a minimum. She hesitated in sitting on any of the seats.

"Please be seated, Lady Edith," Ralph said.

"I know most of the dirt is on the front of my clothing, but I wouldn't wish to get any of it on your lovely fabric. I have no idea what I'm covered in, but it doesn't smell very nice," Edith admitted, her nose wrinkling.

"I'll send a message for your maid to come here and bring a change of clothing," Miles said, moving to the door which led into the hallway.

"Please. Don't worry. Be seated," Ralph said gently.

"Do you have a cover I could use? I would much rather," Edith insisted.

Ralph nodded to his servant, who left the room, but soon returned with a cloth which he placed on a sofa. Edith thanked him before sinking gratefully onto the seat.

Miles had come back into the room. "You can leave us and sort yourself out, Pensby. There's no point delaying. I think we've moved beyond the etiquette of your needing to dance attendance on us whilst we are here."

"Of course. Please help yourself to whatever drinks you wish. Jackson here, will get you anything you need," Ralph said. He'd been watching Edith closely, wanting to say so much and unable to do so.

"I need a brandy!" Edith responded tartly. "I was such a fool."

Ralph smiled at her words. "You're no shrinking miss, Lady Edith. I think even the most experienced young woman would have been taken in by the charms of Mr Sage," he defended her.

"Yes. Even I thought he was up to snuff," Miles admitted.

"You relied on your friend's recommendation," Ralph said.

"Malone is going to rue the day he came back into contact with me," Miles said grimly.

"There's little point in my saying it isn't worth getting into a fight over it, isn't there?" Edith asked.

"In this, I'm afraid, yes," Miles admitted. "He wouldn't expect to get off without retribution. He knows me of old."

"I don't want to see you hurt. Lord Pensby will suffer enough from his fight," Edith said, finally looking at Ralph.

"Stiff knuckles are a small price to pay for teaching that blaggard a lesson," Ralph said roughly.

Edith flushed a little. "It was my stupidity. I shouldn't have climbed into the carriage."

"No. You shouldn't have, but likewise, it wasn't unreasonable to presume he would act the gentleman in an open vehicle in the middle of the street," Miles responded.

Ralph left the brother and sister alone. He had blood on his clothing, which would probably have ruined the fine fabric, but he didn't care. He'd never been as angry in his life as when he'd seen the state of Edith and the look of desperation on her face as she was trying to make her escape. Sage was lucky to be still breathing, because Miles had been wrong. It was worth hanging for to be rid of the person who threatened the woman he loved.

He stilled as his valet helped him out of his clothing. He loved her.

Of course he loved her. He'd known it for weeks, but no matter what his feelings were he still couldn't have her. The more he kept that thought in the forefront of his mind, the better for all of them.

Eventually returning to the drawing room, he was notified that Edith had been taken to his guest chamber and was bathing and changing into clean clothes. He'd taken a large swallow of whisky at the thought of Edith bathing under his roof, but he chided himself at his base thoughts after what she'd been through.

"I'll order my carriage," Ralph offered to Miles. "There's no point forcing your sister to walk, or ride any further. I expect she's more shaken than she appears."

"Yes. She's made of firm stuff, but she was trembling when I first got hold of her," Miles admitted. "Thank you for the thrashing you gave Sage. I owe you a debt of gratitude."

"You would have done the same for me. I couldn't have stood by and watched him get away while you were tending to your sister," Ralph answered.

"I cannot believe how close she came to ruination," Miles admitted. "The thought terrifies me, but what if we hadn't been passing? I suggested Hyde Park, you were the one to offer an alternative. If we'd gone to Hyde Park, we would have been too far away."

"I know," Ralph said quietly. His friend's words did nothing to settle Ralph's temper, which was still bubbling under the surface. He chose the moment to leave the room to order the carriage.

After the servant left the hallway, under Ralph's instructions, Ralph took the moment to let out his breath and run his hand through his hair. She could have so easily been ruined.

"Lord Pensby?" Edith asked tentatively, as she walked into the hallway. She had bathed and changed her clothing and for all intents and purposes looked as if nothing untoward had happened.

"Yes?" Ralph asked in return.

"How are your hands?" Edith asked, crossing the hall and holding out her own hands to take Ralph's.

"There is nothing to worry about," Ralph responded, but placed his hands in hers, nonetheless.

Edith rubbed her thumb over Ralph's knuckles and winced at the already developing bruises and cuts that covered them. "I'm so sorry."

"What for?"

"For being a fool. For causing this. But I thank you from the bottom of my heart that you would do such a thing to protect me. I don't deserve it. I'm quite ashamed of my actions," Edith admitted, her words babbled because of embarrassment and humiliation.

Ralph squeezed her fingers, even though the action caused him pain. "Don't recriminate. It wasn't you at fault. And if my situation were different..."

Edith looked in puzzlement at the unfinished sentence. When it was clear that Ralph wasn't going to continue she spoke. "I don't fully understand."

"I can't explain," Ralph admitted. "But know this, if things were different, if I could be as I would wish… but I can't."

Edith was completely baffled by his words but was sure that he felt the same as she did. She lifted his hands to her lips and kissed each one. The sharp intake of breath was encouragement enough that she hadn't erred.

"Thank you for protecting me. I appreciate it more than I can express," she whispered quietly.

Edith gently let go of one of Ralph's hands and placed her own on his cheek. She was emboldened by the way he closed his eyes and leaned into her touch.

They sprang apart when the servant returned to the hallway and coughed his presence. Edith broke the contact and flushed a deep red, but Ralph shielded her from the prying eyes of the servant.

"Tell Lord Longdon to prepare to leave if the carriage is ready," Ralph growled out.

As the servant entered the drawing room, Ralph bent his head and kissed Edith so quickly, so lightly that afterwards she would almost doubt that it had happened. Then reluctantly he moved away from her to await Miles' entrance.

He was a cad. A devil, but he needed to show her that he cared deeply. Which wasn't fair on her, but he never thought straight when she was in his company, especially when she looked as vulnerable and trusting as she did now.

*

Edith surreptitiously touched her lips as they travelled the short journey to Curzon Street. He had kissed her. She'd hardly been able to respond before Miles had walked into the hall. If he'd seen the kiss, there would have been another whole situation to contend with on what had turned out to be an eventful day, but he hadn't.

She couldn't fathom what it meant. Ralph seemed to want her but then contradicted himself with his words. He sounded like he didn't know what he really wanted, he certainly couldn't speak eloquently on the subject so how she was supposed to guess his feelings was anyone's business.

Miles laid a hand on her arm. "I suggest we don't tell Mother about anything which has occurred today."

"Oh, certainly not!" Edith responded emphatically. "I don't wish to have even further recriminations from her."

"Are you still determined to leave tomorrow?" Miles asked.

"Yes. It's convinced me even more so that I'm not suited to this life. Perhaps one day I'll return to London, but it won't happen for a number of years, if at all," Edith said.

"I still think it's a shame, but I'll support you as much as I can. I will remain in London until Mother decides she'd like to return to Barrowfoot," Miles said.

"I'll hopefully have made some firm plans to establish my own home by then," Edith said.

"There's no hurry. You will have to spend time with Mother in the future, you know," Miles cautioned.

"I know. But I think we both need a break from each other. We have gone through the worst of times recently. Perhaps we just need for life to be less stressful and charged for a little time," Edith responded.

When they reached home, Miles handed her down from the carriage, but went to step back into the vehicle when Edith was on the pavement.

"Where are you going?" Edith asked in surprise.

"I have a score to settle," Miles said. "Don't worry, I'll return soon."

"Oh, no! Leave it, please!" Edith pleaded.

"I can't m'dear," Miles said, gently leaning out of the window and putting his finger under Edith's chin so she looked him directly in the eye. "I have to do this."

Edith gave a slight nod and moved away from the carriage. Her stomach would be in knots until Miles returned safe and well. For now, she had to trust he knew what he was doing and accept that it was something he had to do.

*

It didn't take much effort for Miles to gain access to Albert's rooms. Staff who were not being paid tended to be more amiable to someone handing out a pocket full of coins.

Albert started when Miles entered his drawing room. Miles had purposely walked in nonchalantly, taking off his hat as he entered through the doorway.

"Longdon, I can explain." Albert stood up and faced his old officer.

"I doubt it, but I shall indulge you whilst you try. You can no doubt convince me why you chose my sister for an easy target for that shuffling slyboots, you introduced as a gentleman," Miles said, his tone steely.

"He is a gentleman, but without funds. He did what every other fortune hunter would do," Albert started, trying to defend Mr Sage.

"Every other fortune hunter didn't use their friendship with me to get to my sister," Miles pointed out. "You gave him the means to become closer to Edith than anyone else would normally be allowed. Now, why, after we served together and I thought, respected each other, would you do something like that?"

Albert had the decency to flush a little. "I wouldn't have done so in usual circumstances."

"But you did this time."

"I've fallen on hard times. No war, means no work, means no money. The pittance I receive would hardly keep a dog off the streets," Albert said bitterly.

"And especially not a man with your expensive tastes," Miles spat, looking around the elegantly furnished room.

"No. Not all of us are born to wealth. Charles said he was looking to marry and fell in love with your sister…"

"Oh, spare me the falsehoods! Don't treat me like some sort of nodcock, or I really will kill you today," Miles promised.

Paling slightly, Albert swallowed. "I'm sorry. I didn't think he'd resort to kidnap and forced marriage. That was never part of the plan. As far as I was aware he was intent on charming her into marrying him. He's travelled throughout Europe trying to do the same. No young lady can resist him initially, but he's never secured a marriage with anyone."

"And you decided that through mine and your acquaintance, Edith would be an easy target. When you saw Edith wasn't smitten you didn't think to advise your friend to stay away? Where is he by the way?"

"He took the ship he'd chartered to take himself and Lady Edith to Scotland. He had to be lifted on board, he was in such a bad way," Albert admitted. The sight of Charles had filled him with terror, though he was no coward. He had known what the result would be. He'd actually been preparing to leave, underestimating how soon Miles would be seeking him out. "But, yes I did warn him about continuing to moon after Lady Edith."

"Yet, he didn't listen. Why are you still here? Why didn't you leave with him as I told him to tell you?"

"I was arranging my departure. I just had to plan where I was going. I've parted company with Sage, I didn't agree with what he did and I told him as much," Albert babbled, hoping to save his own skin.

"I hope you did. The fact that you weren't in the coach would suggest you speak the truth, but I'm afraid you're still to be held accountable for bringing him into our midst. You could have quite easily sent a message around to my home today, warning us of the danger Edith faced, yet you chose not to. I'm afraid I cannot let it rest that my sister was taken against her will and had to jump from a moving carriage before being chased and half dragged through the streets of London. You could have prevented that. But you didn't."

Albert tensed at Miles' expression and in a sudden movement threw the table next to him at Miles in an effort to hinder the young man, whilst he made his own escape. Miles ducked aside, avoiding the table and flung himself across a sofa to bring Albert and himself crashing to the ground.

Kicking out, Albert struggled to escape Miles, but although he was fuelled by panic, Miles' motivation gave him the cold edge which he needed. Climbing across Albert, Miles' fist came into contact with Albert's stomach. As Albert retaliated, Miles blocked blows while delivering those of his own.

When he was satisfied that Albert wouldn't forget the consequences of betraying his trust anytime soon, Miles stood and brushed himself off.

"You should have left with Sage," he said coldly, looking down at the prone form. Albert watched his attacker warily, half expecting another beating, but Miles had made his point. "I suggest you disappear into a hole and don't come back anytime soon."

"Where am I to go?" Albert bleated. "I have no money."

"I suggest you get yourself abroad. I'm sure there are openings for sneaky, untrustworthy scoundrels like you," Miles said with derision. "But one thing's for sure, I'll be letting the whole battalion know what trick you've pulled on one of your own. I doubt you'll get a welcome from anyone in London anytime soon."

"You've as good as made me destitute!" Albert cried out.

Miles bent forward, at which Albert winced. "No. You and your friend did that when you tried to harm my family." Miles stood straight once more and reached for his hat.

"He's the best offer she's ever likely to get, the dried up, sour ape-leader that she is!" Albert said, anger making him foolish.

In one swift movement, Miles punched Albert in the gut. After watching him writhe in pain for a moment, he placed his hat on his head and walked through the doorway without looking back.

Chapter 14

My Dear Miss S,
Have you ever done something that you really want to even though you know it's wrong? For once, I forgot what I should do and now I feel like I have behaved poorly towards a person who is dear to me. I can't regret my actions for even just for the briefest of moments. It gave me a glimpse of a life I might have had if my circumstances were different.

I do not repine. I don't wish you to feel sorry for me. I accept the decisions I've made as the right things to do, but recently, I've had cause to imagine a different path and it has rattled my equilibrium.

Life has been eventful recently, surprising for one who avoids it as best I can. I thought I was immune to people, but it appears not. I can fight for what is right, something I didn't believe to be true.

I have to return home soon and I think that is when our correspondence should end. I need to face my future and you need to plan for yours. Believe me when I say, I know without doubt that you deserve to be loved wholeheartedly by a man worthy of you. I wish I could be that person.

Miss S, you are a delight. Don't let anyone try to convince you otherwise.
Kindest regards,
Mr S

Edith read and reread the letter, the frown never leaving her face. Eventually, she placed it into her portmanteau which was packed and ready to be carried to the carriage. When the letter was safely away, she moved to the fireplace and stood looking down into it.

Miles entered Edith's bedchamber and noticed her frowning stance. "What is it, m'dear? Having second thoughts?"

Startled a little, Edith turned a smile on her face. "No, not at all, but I would like to speak to Lord Pensby before I leave. Could you escort me to his lodgings, please?"

"Why do you want to see Pensby?"

"I need to see him after yesterday. I want to thank him properly and to check he is well," Edith improvised.

"You can send a note round for that. No need to go to his home and disturb him," Miles responded.

"Miles, please. Take me to him," Edith cajoled.

"I'm not a fool, Edith. I've seen the way you look at Ralph. I've warned you before, he isn't the marrying kind," Miles cautioned.

"It's not about marrying him! Just indulge me in this, I think he needs his friends. It's a feeling, a niggle, an educated guess – call it what you will, but I need you to go around to where he is staying, even if you won't take me and check he is well," Edith insisted.

Miles let out a long-suffering sigh. "Fine. You remain here though. It'll be easier for him to confess to me if there is something wrong, which of course there isn't."

Edith had to be content with her brother's decision, but she would be on tenterhooks until Miles returned.

*

Miles stepped up to Ralph's front door and immediately gave some credit to Edith's feelings, as the knocker had been removed from the door. His friend hadn't mentioned leaving London, which he always did.

Miles banged on the door in case any member of staff had been left behind. Just as he was about to leave, a young servant opened the door cautiously.

"When did Lord Pensby leave?" Miles demanded not unkindly.

"This morning, m'lud."

"When does he return?"

"It depends on how well Lady Pensby is," the servant answered.

"Lady Pensby? Is she ill?" Miles tried to hide the fact that he knew nothing about Ralph's mother, let alone she suffered from an illness.

"Yes, although, Mr Jackson says that the new treatment seems to be working. Which is good news."

"It is indeed," Miles answered. "I have business with Lord Pensby, but nothing urgent, I will see him when he returns. Here's my card." Having handed over the elegantly printed card, Miles stepped back onto the pavement.

As he retraced his steps to Curzon Street, he pondered over everything Ralph had ever told him about his family. He had very little to go on, which he suddenly felt ashamed about.

Entering the hallway of his own abode, he went straight into the drawing room when told his sister was waiting for him there. As soon as he entered Edith stood to greet him.

"What news? Your frown would suggest you aren't going to deliver good tidings," Edith said.

"He's well, as far as I know," Miles said quickly. "But I've just had it brought home to me how little I actually know Pensby."

"Why? What's happened?" Edith asked.

Miles related the information he'd gleaned. "I didn't know his mother was ill. I knew she was alive, and I suspected there might be some condition or other which prevented her from travelling to London, but he hardly ever spoke about her at all. I've no idea what ails her, but if it's the reason Ralph is always leaving London, it must be something serious."

"He's gone home," Edith mused. She thought for a few moments and then turned to her brother. "We need to go to him."

"What? No! He wouldn't appreciate our interference," Miles said quickly.

"Who is there to support Lord Pensby? Has he any other family? Close friends? Anyone he could call on for support?" Edith asked.

"Not that I know of," Miles admitted. "I'm his closest friend as far as I know."

"When we were in need of good friends yesterday, he helped without question or hesitation. In fact, he went above and beyond what most friends would be prepared to do," Edith pointed out.

"Yes. He did."

"Now, it's our turn," Edith said. "I have you and that thought got me through the worst of days over the last few years. Even though you weren't there in person, I could write to you and garner support from your letters. I wouldn't have known who to turn to or how to seek assistance if you hadn't been there."

"You did amazingly well," Miles conceded.

"Thank you. But if Lord Pensby hasn't got anyone to take his part, who does he turn to in times of real despair?" Edith asked.

"Men are different," Miles answered. "We don't ask for help, or need it. We just get on with what has to be faced."

"That is the most nonsensical thing I think I've ever heard you utter!" Edith scolded. "Everyone needs help sometimes. It doesn't matter whether one is a man or woman. Without support we all can flounder."

Miles had flushed slightly at Edith's words. "Fine, I accept what you say. But there's nothing we can do if Ralph doesn't ask for help."

"Oh, is there not?" Edith asked, a gleam in her eye.

"Edith, I'm not going along with any more of your foolish schemes, so forget what you are about to say!" Miles responded quickly.

"That's fine, but if you think I am about to abandon the man who jumped in to protect me without pause, or a thought for his own welfare, you don't know me so well!"

"You're bloody-minded, has anyone ever told you that?"

Edith smiled sweetly. "It's no wonder my language is appalling with you as my example."

"What do you think we should do?" Miles asked, resigned.

"Mother won't be happy, but I think you should accompany me and although we'll go home we'll call at the Pensby home on our way," Edith said, pleased that Miles was finally persuadable to her scheme.

"And the fact that Barrowfoot and Lymewood are in opposite directions?" Miles asked, raising his eyebrows at his sister.

"A minor detail," Edith waved away his point. "If he has concerns on his mind such as his mother's health, a little detail like we are heading in the wrong direction won't be noticed."

"You don't get to be a successful gamester like Pensby is, by not noticing every tiny detail, I assure you."

"Hmm. Fair point. We shall just have to invent a relative we are going to see. For a companion for me! Perfect. You must always hide a lie in a truth," Edith said pleased with herself.

"You really do worry me sometimes, Edith. You really do," Miles said with a shake of the head.

"All you need to concern yourself with is persuading Mother that she can do without you for a few days," Edith said with a chuckle. "I don't envy you that conversation, but as she isn't speaking to me I can't volunteer to have it in your stead. You always find a way to bring her around to your way of thinking though, so I'm sure you'll be up to the task."

"And who do I suggest that she ask to stay here with her? Because she won't remain here alone," Miles pointed out.

"No. I've thought about that. If she invites Miss Robinson and Miss Webster to stay for a week or so, she will have two perfect ladies to console her about what a poor situation she has. They can all agree that she has two ungrateful brats, who neglect her terribly. She'll be ecstatic," Edith responded, having thought through the whole scheme.

"I'm sure we're not related," Miles said shaking his head and standing. "I could never be as conniving as you appear to be."

"It's a case of needs must, dear brother. It's all for a worthy cause in the end," Edith said angelically.

"And what's the cause?"

"To help a friend in need," Edith said, as Miles left the room. "And secure myself the only man I could possibly marry, who's been writing to me," she whispered as the door closed.

Chapter 15

Edith looked out of the carriage window as it approached the village of Sandiford. It had been surprisingly easy to persuade Lady Longdon that she would be better off in the company of her friends for a few weeks than that of her children. The friends would agree with anything her ladyship gave an opinion of. Added to the fact their accommodation and food would be of a far higher quality than they were wont to eat at home, it was a perfect situation for them as well.

Miles had set off a little perturbed that he could so easily be replaced in his mother's affections. Edith had teased him that his sense of self-importance had overestimated their mother's maternal feelings.

Now, in the early evening they were entering the village which was only a mile or so away from Lymewood, the seat of the Pensby family.

The Red Lion was the best posting house in the village and the innkeeper was happy to have two of the best rooms rented by members of the Quality. Being so close to London, many people continued further before breaking their journey so overnight visitors weren't as common as the innkeeper and his lady would have liked.

Once settled in and refreshed, Edith left her maid in her chamber and joined Miles in a private parlour. They sat to a warming meal of beef stew, lamb fillets and venison pie.

"I should go and see Ralph alone in the first instance," Miles said, once they had made great inroads into the hearty meal.

"Oh no. He will easily bamboozle you into believing that everything is right and tight," Edith said. "It will require the tact of a woman to get us in."

Miles let out a crack of laughter. "You, my dear, are about as subtle as the Prince Regent's waist."

"Miles! That's a terrible thing to say," Edith gurgled with laughter. "I'm not so outrageous as you make out. And I assure you, you will need me there."

"If I insist I go alone?"

"I'll just go for a walk and if I happen on the parkland of Lymewood, who's to say if I get lost..."

"I don't know why I bother to argue. It's easier just to agree in the first instance," Miles groaned.

Edith smiled. "You are such a good brother."

"I'm a pushover."

*

Edith wasn't feeling quite as confident as she'd sounded the evening before, once they were trundling along the driveway to Lymewood. She looked out of the window and chewed her lip as she anticipated what sort of reaction their arrival might cause.

Stepping down from the carriage, she was able to admire the red-brick Jacobean building which was the Pensby seat. It had ten windows either side of a large portico, which was clearly a more recent addition. The house was a contrast to Edith's own home, which was a recently refurbished home in the Palladian style.

The door was answered by the butler and after Miles had explained their visit and where they had travelled from, the servant showed them into an anteroom off the hallway.

"Lady Pensby is not receiving visitors," the butler explained to them. "Neither is Lord Pensby at this time, but as you have travelled so far, I will take your card to him."

"This is a bad idea," Miles hissed at his sister when they were left alone.

"I know," Edith agreed.

"Good God," Miles muttered before starting to pace the floorspace of the room, his boots seeming to make an inordinate amount of noise in the quiet house.

Both looked up expectantly when they heard footsteps coming down the stairs, but it was the butler who reappeared, not Ralph.

"Lord Pensby has asked me to show you into the drawing room. He will be with you in a few moments. I have ordered tea to be brought to you," the butler said, turning to lead the way up the stairs to the first-floor room.

When they were shown into the magnificent large bright space, Edith smiled at her brother. "We've made it through the door, that's a good start," she said, her confidence a little stronger. "He could have refused us entry."

"There's still time for him to throw us out," Miles answered darkly.

It was around ten minutes before Ralph appeared at the door. He looked tired and one of his hands was wrapped in a dressing.

"Longdon, Lady Edith. What are you doing here?" he asked roughly; there was no welcome in his eyes.

Miles looked at Edith expectantly and with a grim look of 'I told you so' in his expression.

Edith swallowed. This was not how she'd imagined their reception would be. Noticing the dressing on Ralph's hand and the way he avoided using the hand as he'd entered the room, her hesitation only lasted for a second.

"Oh, your hand! I knew you'd be injured from the fight, I just knew it! I had to see you for myself," she said crossing over to Ralph. "Did you ride here, or take your carriage?"

"I rode," Ralph answered, a little dumbfounded at her reaction to his cool greeting.

"You foolish, foolish man! Why would you put your hand under so much strain? If you'd have travelled by carriage, you could have rested it. Are the cuts not healing?"

Ralph looked at Miles, as if seeking his assistance, but Miles wisely just shrugged and left Ralph to his sister's ministrations.

"I don't think so," Ralph said, trying to hide his hand from Edith, but his movement caused her to reach out and grab it.

"I must see your injuries. They must be bathed and properly cleaned. You can't risk an infection."

"It'll be fine," Ralph muttered.

"I'll be the decider of that!" Edith said tartly. "Please allow me to ring the bell. I need some items if I'm to tend you."

"I'd rather you didn't," Ralph said gruffly.

Edith paused. Looking into Ralph's eyes was like looking into two deep pools of chocolate. He was trying to hide from her, she knew it, but he couldn't hide well enough. "Please," she said quietly.

Ralph nodded, closing his eyes for the briefest moment. He didn't want her here. He didn't want to be anywhere near her because when he was, he longed for her and that didn't do either of them any good. Yet, it seemed he couldn't refuse her anything.

Edith waited near the fireplace until the butler entered. "Could you please bring me a bowl of warm water, cloths and fresh dressing for his lordship. I'll also need some brandy and honey," she instructed.

If the butler was surprised at being given such orders by one of the strangers, who his master had cursed to the devil when he'd been told of their presence, he didn't show it. Instead he bowed slightly and left the room.

"I knew it was the right decision to come here," Edith said, ignoring the snort from her brother. "You would have neglected the wound and probably died of an infection! It isn't brave to not attend to yourself you know."

"Is she always this damned annoying?" Ralph asked Miles.

"She's actually getting worse," Miles admitted.

"Brats," Edith responded, not taking the slightest offence at the insults.

As soon as the butler returned with a tray full of the requested items, Edith got to work. Unwrapping the bandage, she winced at the cuts which looked red and swollen.

"If you feel queasy..." Ralph started to say at her reaction.

"I grew up with three brothers, I'm not in the least inclined to nausea. I've seen plenty of gore over the years. Charles, in particular was prone to fall out of trees. Why the stupid boy continued to climb them, goodness only knows," Edith explained briskly. "I'm just aware that these injuries were gained because of my actions. It's almost as if I've inflicted them on you myself."

"My fist would have had a softer target if I would be dastardly enough to punch you," Ralph responded.

"Is that your way of telling me I'm fat, Lord Pensby? That's very ungentlemanly of you."

"N-no, I—" Ralph stuttered, but stopped when he saw the twinkle of amusement in Edith's eyes. "Termagant," he whispered.

Edith surprised him into a groan as, without warning she poured a liberal amount of brandy over his open wound.

"What a waste of decent brandy," Miles muttered from across the room.

"Go to the devil!" Ralph said, gritting his teeth as the alcohol stung his injuries.

"Be brave," Edith said with a laugh in her voice. "The next stage will be better. She patted around the area until the brandy had dried and then covered the wounds with honey.

"What are you doing now?" Ralph asked.

"Father always said that honey provided a barrier which stopped infection. I've no idea where he got the idea from, but it seemed to work with my brothers whilst they were growing. A pity it couldn't help them at the end," Edith explained.

"The downside is you smell like some sort of lightskirt's cheap perfume," Miles interjected with a chuckle.

"For God's sake, Longdon! Your sister is in the room!" Ralph expostulated.

"I'm also used to base language," Edith said. "And have been known to use it a time or two. I'm afraid I'm no simpering miss, which is part of the reason I would never have been a hit at any season. Even when I was straight out of the schoolroom. I'm a lost cause."

Ralph looked as if to speak, but instead his lips set in a grim line. He didn't utter anything else, until Edith had replaced his bandage with a clean one and sat back satisfied with her work.

"There! That's better," she said with a smile.

"Thank you, but there really was no need," Ralph said gruffly.

"You should have stopped at thank you," Edith chided. "There's nothing nice about receiving a polite acceptance of a service, to then finish with a derogatory comment."

Ralph looked at Miles as he stood to move away from Edith, but his friend just shrugged and laughed.

"Don't appeal to me. I'd still be in London if I had any authority over her," Miles admitted.

Edith calmly poured tea for Ralph and handed the cup to him which he mutely accepted. Once the cup was emptied, he spoke. "Thank you for coming, your consideration is appreciated. I'm afraid I'm not in a position to offer further hospitality."

"That's fine," Miles said, rising. "Edith is going to Barrowfoot. This was a short diversion."

"Of a few days," Edith interjected. "We will be staying in the village, at the Red Lion, and I hope you will allow me to check on your hand in a day or two. I would hate to leave thinking everything was well and then to find out you'd caught an infection after all. I would have been happier if you had cared for the injuries from the start. By neglecting them, it's just increased my concern."

"Edith!" Miles said exasperated.

"I don't need entertaining, or hand-holding, so you can explore the countryside to your heart's content, brother. I will read in our rooms," Edith said primly.

"And if you believe that, you're a bigger fool than I am," Ralph aimed at his friend. "I shall call on you tomorrow, Lady Edith. It is best that way."

"As you wish," Edith said regally, standing before curtseying to Ralph.

The brother and sister were shown out, leaving Ralph standing in the middle of the room. Rubbing his uninjured hand over his face, he let out a breath of confused frustration.

"What the devil is she trying to do to me?" he asked the room in general, before turning to what was left of the brandy and swallowing it in one gulp straight from the decanter.

Chapter 16

Lady Pensby was seated in the window seat in her sitting room when Ralph entered the room. Smiling he walked over and kissed his mother's cheek.

"How are you?" he asked, his usual question on first seeing her.

"I'm feeling excellent. I'm going to venture downstairs today," came the answer.

"Do you think that's wise?"

"I wouldn't have said it if I didn't," Lady Pensby smiled at her son. "You do treat me as if I have some sort of death wish, which I don't."

Ralph sat next to his mother. "I know. But I worry. You're precious to me."

"As you are to me, my love. But you can't keep me cosseted forever. That isn't the type of life I wish to have, as you wouldn't wish it either," she said gently.

"No."

"I hear there have been visitors to the house," Lady Pensby said with an arch expression.

"Bloody gossiping servants," Ralph muttered, at which his mother laughed.

"Yes. Thank God for them, or my days would be very tedious," Lady Pensby defended her loyal staff. "So, who were they? And why didn't you send a message for me to come and meet them. We have so few visitors these days, it's cruel to keep any we do have away from me."

"You are too unwell to be tiring yourself out on callers," Ralph said.

Lady Pensby's face darkened. "Don't you dare try and dictate to me!" she said roughly.

"Please don't upset yourself," Ralph said quickly.

"Don't act like some sort of tyrant and I won't," Lady Pensby responded. "Now, I want to know all the details."

"I'm surrounded by managing women!" Ralph growled out, before explaining who Miles and Edith were.

"Finally, I get to hear the real reason your hand was bandaged. To say it was caught in a door was a poor lie which I should take you to task over. They sound like good friends," Lady Pensby said after hearing about the long-time friendship. "I'm glad you defended Lady Edith. What a cad this Mr Sage sounds."

"Of the worse kind," Ralph said, gritting his teeth at how close Edith had come to ruination.

"I'd like to meet them. I've met so few of the people you have associated with over the years."

"That's because I have few acquaintances and even fewer people who I would consider as friends," Ralph said with a smile.

"An even better reason to meet these two friends then," Lady Pensby persisted.

"They won't be visiting again. I've made it clear that we aren't entertaining. They're going on to their own home soon, this was a short diversion."

"They leave tomorrow?"

"No. In a day or two, I believe. I've said, I'll call on them before they leave."

"Send them my regards, won't you?" Lady Pensby asked.

"Of course. Now you rest. I'll pop in later to see how you are," Ralph said, standing and kissing his mother's hand.

"Yes. I'll certainly rest," Lady Pensby said. Watching her son leave the room, she stood and walked to her desk. Sitting down she took out a piece of paper and dipped her quill into the ink. Glancing at the door, she started to write, a smile playing on her lips.

*

"I do think it's a mistake remaining here," Miles said as he pulled on his gloves. "But if you're determined to act like a lovesick moonling, who am I to stop you?"

"You can be a blasted nuisance sometimes," Edith retorted. "I'm being nothing of the sort."

"It is I who will have to mop up your tears, dear sister, when it all ends in disaster," Miles pointed out, not unreasonably. "For you won't secure him."

"Pfft! You know nothing," Edith said with derision. "Now go on your ride with Lord Pensby. You can both talk about how neither of you wish to be married because you're both so happy not being attached to the women you love and who love you in return. One day you might actually convince each other that you speak the truth, but I doubt it."

Miles looked a little stunned at Edith's words, but didn't respond. Her words had struck a little too close for comfort for one of his usual flippant responses. Instead he bowed his head slightly. "I shall see you in an hour or two," he said stiffly, before leaving the room.

Edith shook her head at her brother's retreating form. "At least I have hope for Lord Pensby. You, dear brother, need a horse kick to knock you in the right direction. You fool. She'd be perfect for you but she won't be allowed to remain single forever."

Picking up her book, she sat in the chair nearest the fire. She could have insisted that she accompany her brother and Ralph on their horse ride, but for once, she thought it would be detrimental to her cause. He would come in afterwards, she was sure, so at least she would have a little time with him, she would have to content herself with that.

After only ten minutes of uninterrupted reading, she was disturbed by a knock on the door. A maid brought in a note and waited for a response.

Opening the letter, Edith couldn't help the smile spreading across her face.

Dear Lady Edith,

My son did not introduce us yesterday, for which he has received a motherly rebuke. I know he is overprotective, as I have the unfortunate curse of being in poor health, but I'm not as much an invalid as my son pretends I am. He does it with the best of intentions, so I do forgive him, mostly.

I hear you are to leave the area soon and hope you can visit me this afternoon, to share some tea and cakes and a little gossip. I long for some female company, who can tell me the latest on dits of the season. It isn't the same reading everything from newspapers. We have so few people passing through, I would appreciate even a little of your time if you can spare it.

I shall expect you at two of the clock, if you are not otherwise engaged. A simple message to say you accept my invitation is all I require.

Please come.
Yours,
Lady Pensby.

Edith looked up. "Please send a message, that I shall attend and prepare my carriage for leaving at half past the hour."

Ralph would kill her if he knew. She knew without a doubt, but how could she refuse such a request? Promising herself she would only stay fifteen minutes, she put her book to one side to prepare for her unexpected visit.

*

Edith was shown into Lady Pensby's sitting room. The room wasn't as grand as the main drawing room, but it was a space which was homely and tastefully furnished. Lady Pensby stood to greet Edith at her entrance.

"Hello, my dear. I'm so glad you decided to join me," she said in welcome.

"Oh, you are so like your son!" Edith exclaimed. "I do beg your pardon. I shouldn't be so impertinent," she said with a blush.

Lady Pensby laughed. "I can't be offended by something which is obviously true." She was as dark as her son, but her eyes glittered with amusement. Her skin was pallid, but her eyes and smile were warm. "Come, sit with me. I want to know all about you."

Edith was a little daunted by the comment. She had no idea what, if anything, Ralph had told his mother and so sat with feelings of trepidation. Her hostess seemed to sense her hesitation and changed the subject.

"I promise not to utter a word of what we share," Lady Pensby promised. "But I'm hoping you can give me an insight into how my son spends his time in London."

"I can't tell you much I'm afraid, he doesn't spend a lot of his time in society," Edith admitted. She couldn't utter outrageous lies. "But I can confirm he is a good dancing partner and I owe him a great debt."

"Ah. Yes. I hope you don't mind that Ralph spoke of the escapade. He couldn't really avoid it when I saw he was injured. He didn't condemn you for a moment though. What an absolute rake you had the misfortune to meet!"

Edith had flushed with embarrassment. "I pride myself on being a good judge of character, but I was no better than a green girl when climbing into the carriage with him. It has me staring at the canopy of my bed every night, cursing myself."

"But this is your first season, my dear! How could you be fully up to snuff, as Ralph always says? I believe even your brother was taken in, and I'm presuming he's no raw youth. How can you condemn yourself when a hardened military man was fooled?" Lady Pensby asked.

Edith smiled at the term Lady Pensby had used. Her mother would have been mortified to hear it on a lady of rank's lips. "I don't mind learning a hard lesson, but wish that Lord Pensby and my brother hadn't been put to so much trouble."

"I would think less of them if they hadn't done anything about a man trying to take advantage of a young woman, especially one as pretty as you are."

"With regards to my brother, to be sure, but not Lord Pensby. He shouldn't have been dragged into the situation," Edith said.

"I think my son wouldn't have had it any other way. And not just because he's a gentleman," Lady Pensby said gently.

Edith looked warily at her hostess, but her gaze was met with a smile.

"Can we be honest with each other, my dear?" Lady Pensby asked, picking up one of Edith's hands and squeezing it gently between both of her frailer ones.

"Y-yes," Edith stuttered.

"I know Ralph hides from society and it saddens me that my illness keeps him from making friends and enjoying flirtations. His life has been far too serious for my liking. Duty and responsibility should come later in life, not when one is young, as Ralph was when he inherited the title," Lady Pensby explained.

"I'm sure he does not begrudge a single moment," Edith said quickly.

"It's to his credit that he doesn't," Lady Pensby said. "That isn't to say I don't curse every time he is sent for because of me. I promise to remain quiet so he can enjoy his life. I'm constantly persuading him to take off and go to London, to forget about me and homelife for a while. To just be a young man."

"It is a poor situation for you both to be in. Equally torn in your efforts to try and do the best by each other," Edith said, gaining more of an insight into Ralph's life.

"Yes. I hope to see you lots whilst you are in the area. I don't have many visitors and hope you shall visit every day," Lady Pensby said.

"We'll see," Edith said doubtfully. "Now it is time I left you. I don't want to overtax you, or I will warrant the scolding which would surely come my way."

"You're starting to treat me as invalidish as my son does!"

"And rightly so if you allow yourself to become exhausted," Edith responded, standing. "It has been a pleasure to meet you and I hope my visit won't tire you too much."

"Not in the slightest. It has made me feel better than I have in a long time," Lady Pensby said honestly, but she didn't try to detain Edith. When her visitor had left her, she rested her head on the back of the sofa. "Oh, Ralph, you've picked out someone who's perfect for you. You clever, clever boy."

Chapter 17

Edith wasn't surprised to receive another letter the following morning. Unfortunately, Miles was in the parlour when it was delivered. There was no chance that Edith would convince him it was from someone back in London, especially when the maid said the letter had come from the big house.

Flushing, Edith had held her hands up defensively. "Don't condemn me! For once, this isn't my doing."

"I wait with dread for an explanation," Miles responded grimly.

"Yesterday, I received a note from Lady Pensby, inviting me to take tea with her," Edith explained. "I hadn't attempted to make any contact with her, in fact I was astounded to receive it."

"But you chose not to mention it, either before or after you went?" Miles asked.

"Well, no," Edith admitted. "I thought it best to go and see her myself as she requested."

"Pensby wouldn't have agreed to it, if he'd known anything about it."

"No. But, Miles, she's a lovely woman and so lonely!" Edith said quickly. "She says she sees no one at all and relies on staff to give her the latest gossip."

Miles ran his hands through his hair. "Edith, you are playing with fire," he ground out. "Yesterday, Pensby opened up a little about his mother and his concerns. She can be very ill and the spasms she suffers from come on suddenly. How would you feel if one came on whilst you were there? How would Pensby feel? For he's convinced that exertion brings them on. There's no doubt in my mind that he would blame you if anything happened to his mother whilst you were in her presence."

Miles' words did nothing to ease Edith's own guilt at deceiving Ralph. She was torn, for she genuinely liked Lady Pensby and pitied her situation. It also pandered to a little of her own vanity, pleased that the mother of the man she loved seemed to like her.

"I think it's time we left this place," Miles said. "We're going home tomorrow. I'd say today, but I don't wish to make Ralph suspect what you've been doing," Miles said. "I would ask that you don't go to pay a visit to Lady Pensby though. I think it's the wrong thing to do for many reasons."

"Yes. I think it's right to leave here," Edith acknowledged. "I'll send a letter of regret to Lady Pensby."

"Good," Miles responded.

Edith immediately sat at the small desk in the room and wrote a short note. Ringing for the maid, she asked for it to be sent to Lady Pensby.

"There. For once, I've been sensible," she said with a smile at her brother.

"Are you coming for a ride with us?" Miles asked.

"No. I think I'll go for a walk, but I won't go far from the inn. I'll take my maid, don't worry," Edith said easily.

"No mischief?"

"No. Not this time," Edith responded with a smile.

"I suppose I'll have to be content with that," Miles said.

*

Returning back to the inn after a relaxing walk through the lanes surrounding the village, Edith was surprised to see the Pensby carriage in the inn's yard. Hurrying inside, she was greeted by the innkeeper who informed her that Lady Pensby was awaiting her arrival in her private parlour.

"Good God!" Edith exclaimed. "What is she thinking?"

Not waiting for an answer from the innkeeper she hurried into the room. Sitting regally on one of the chairs near to the fire was Lady Pensby, looking elegant, but very frail.

"My Lady! You shouldn't have travelled here! What would your son say?" Edith was worried enough to speak openly.

Lady Pensby smiled. "But you would not come to me, my dear. And I so wanted to see you."

"Oh, my dear Lady Pensby, you should have sent a further note. Please don't stay here. What if you're taken ill? I would never forgive myself," Edith said, wringing her hands. She felt truly afraid that the journey would prove too much for the ailing woman.

"I have been so well recently, I'm sure it will be fine, but just let me finish my tea and then I will leave. I don't want to cause you any distress. Be seated child and stop worrying. You are as bad as Ralph," Lady Pensby said.

"I can understand why he worries," Edith admitted, her heart still pounding with fear. She sat on the edge of the chair, ready to jump up if needed. She had no idea what she'd be able to do if her guest was taken ill. The thought terrified her.

"He can't protect me all of the time."

"No. But when one has a small family and has lost so many other members, the few that are left become even more treasured," Edith explained. "My brother, especially, is so precious to me, for I have lost my father and two brothers."

"I do understand, but that is one of the reasons I encourage Ralph to spend time in company. I wish to see my son married, so his family will grow," Lady Pensby countered.

A fleeting image of brown-eyed children was pushed aside by Edith; she couldn't long for something which wasn't possible. "I'm sure he'll marry when he wants to. My brother says he considers himself too young to marry, perhaps Lord Pensby feels the same?"

"No. There are other thoughts churning inside of Ralph. I know my son and know he is set against marriage for a foolish reason, he's decided can't be overcome. I'd hoped I could recruit you to help me to change his mind."

"I'm not sure what I could do, your son his is own man. I know what my own brother's opinion would be if he found out I was trying to encourage him to choose a wife. Apart from that, I'm afraid I'm leaving tomorrow, so I can't really be of any practical help," Edith said.

"That's a real pity. I was looking forward to your company for days to come," Lady Pensby looked crestfallen.

"I'm afraid it can't be helped," Edith said. It was the right decision. Somehow being with Lady Pensby had shown her she was chasing an unachievable dream. Ralph didn't want to fix his interest with her and the sooner she accepted that, the better.

Lady Pensby stood. "My dear, it has been a pleasure to meet you and I do hope our paths cross again one day," she said, holding out her hand to Edith.

Edith walked with Lady Pensby to her carriage and waited until the carriage door was closed. Stepping back she smiled and waved, before noticing that Miles and Ralph had entered the yard on their horses.

Colouring, but not allowing herself to feel guilty; she had encouraged Lady Pensby to leave, after all. She gave one last wave, nodded to the gentlemen, then turned on her heel and entered the inn.

Her heart was pounding but she stood in front of the fireplace, expecting to see Ralph bursting through the door at any moment. When only Miles entered, she nearly sagged with relief.

"I see you found a way of getting around what we agreed," Miles said stiffly. "You do realise that Pensby has gone charging home in a real temper."

"It does depress me slightly that you are prone to look on the black side of anything to do with me," Edith said tartly.

"Experience has taught me to do so," Miles replied with a shrug, taking a seat opposite where Edith still stood.

"Well for your information, dear brother, I went for a walk, with my maid, just as I said I would. When I returned Lady Pensby was waiting for me. I was horrified to realise she'd travelled here, I assure you."

"From Pensby's reaction, I don't think she has left the house for years," Miles said, unable to repeat the language that Ralph had actually used.

"No one was as shocked as I, honestly," Edith responded. "In fact, I think I was quite rude, because I all but chivvied her out of the door in my hurry to see her return home. The poor woman asked to be allowed to finish her tea before she left. If I hadn't been so worried, I'd have been ashamed at my behaviour."

Miles shook his head. "Pensby was angrier than I've ever seen him. We'll probably be able to hear his cursings from here when he speaks to her."

"I hope he doesn't act like a brute in front of his mother," Edith said hotly. "She'll need quiet and rest when she returns home and hopefully, there'll be no after-effects from her exertion."

*

Ralph had paced in his chamber, his hands balled into fists, raging inside as he tried to calm himself down before seeing his mother. It was a full hour before he had himself under enough control, but his jaw ached at the attempt to remain steadfast in his desire not to lose his temper.

Entering his mother's bedchamber, his anger receded as, to his dismay she was already in bed. "Mother, do you ail?"

"No, my dear boy, but I've had an exciting day, so thought it prudent to rest."

"I saw your carriage leaving the inn," Ralph said.

"Ah, I thought I glimpsed you, but I wasn't sure," Lady Pensby said pleasantly. "I like your friend's sister."

"And how did you come to meet Lady Edith?" Ralph asked coolly.

"Am I to be scolded?" came the amused question. "I didn't think our roles had changed quite so far. Am I no longer the parent?"

Ralph gritted his teeth. "I'm curious to know why you met with Lady Edith and why you thought travelling in the carriage was a good idea."

"It wasn't a good idea, it was a grand adventure!" Lady Pensby laughingly replied. "Oh, my dear boy, stop trying to hide the scowl on your face. The expression you are wearing isn't becoming. Now sit by me and I'll tell you all about it."

Ralph reluctantly sat on the edge of the bed and listened as his mother told of her escapades since the day before. When Lady Pensby had finished extoling the virtues of Lady Edith, she lay back on her pillows. "You see, I'm being very sensible and resting and there have been no ill effects. I do believe it was worth the little bit of risk, for it was such a lovely feeling to escape for a short while."

"Mother, you are precious to me, please don't take such risks in future," Ralph pleaded.

"Lady Edith said it was hard when one had such a small family. I suppose it's different for me, because I know it is natural for me to leave you at some point in your life. Lady Edith understood why you would be angry with me. Do you know she wouldn't rest easy until I was back in my carriage? The child was virtually bouncing in her seat when I refused to leave."

"That's something I suppose," Ralph muttered darkly.

"Now, now, Ralph, don't start blaming the wrong person. It was all my doing. I imposed on a young lady, who clearly was worried about my wellbeing. I did feel a trifle guilty, but I couldn't completely feel conscience-stricken because I had so much enjoyment travelling out of the grounds. Don't take that away from me with dark looks and quiet mutterings," Lady Pensby chided.

"But if they hadn't come to the area on some trumped-up reason, none of this would have happened."

"And I would have missed out on meeting the delightful Lady Edith. I do like her. Don't you?"

Ralph refused to answer, but reached over to kiss his mother. "Rest now. There has been far too much excitement for my liking."

"Oh pfft," Lady Pensby responded, but didn't force the point she'd been trying to make. She was fully aware that if she pushed too far, Ralph would rail against her out of bloody-mindedness.

Ralph left the room and indicated to his footman. "Send a message to prepare the carriage. I'm going out."

Chapter 18

Edith was apprehensive when Ralph was shown into their parlour. She'd known he would come and, in some ways, his arrival was preferable to the waiting. Now he was here and her stomach started to knot. His eyes blazed even if he had the appearance of calm.

"Longdon, Lady Edith," Ralph bowed stiffly.

Miles stood. "I don't want an argument, Pensby," he said quietly.

"I just want a word with your sister," Ralph said coolly.

"Miles, leave us be," Edith said. "This is because of my actions. I don't wish you to be dragged into a dispute between myself and your friend."

Miles shrugged and walked to the door. "I shall enjoy a cigar whilst walking down the lane," he said. "I don't expect to hear raised voices."

With the warning given, he left the room. The two combatants faced each other, one angry, one wary.

"Do you have no consideration about your impact on other people's lives, or is it just my life you insist on interfering with?" Ralph snapped.

Edith winced. "I'm sorry your mother came out here today. I wasn't easy until she was on her way home. I never for a moment thought she would drive here when I sent my apologies to her."

"But you went to Lymewood yesterday."

"Yes. I didn't see any harm in that and I made sure to only stay for fifteen minutes," Edith said defensively.

"You didn't consider that the exertion a visit would cause my mother was enough a reason to deter you?"

"Is Lady Pensby ill?" Edith asked, immediately stepping towards Ralph.

"No, but she returned to bed, exhausted when she got home today."

"But she hasn't had one of her episodes?"

"No," Ralph reluctantly admitted.

"Oh, thank goodness," Edith said with relief, her hand unconsciously coming to rest on her heart.

"Why did you really come here? The reason you gave was flimsy at best," Ralph changed the subject. He was staring at Edith intently. She wasn't sure if he was going to throttle her, but there certainly seemed some difficulty in restraining himself.

"I came to see you," Edith admitted, her shoulders slumping.

"Yes, you explained it was to see if I was well, but that was a ridiculous excuse. What was the real reason?" Ralph persisted.

Edith flushed and chewed her lip. She noticed Ralph watching her lips and flushed even more. "I wanted to see you," she repeated.

Ralph looked as if he were going to explode but then paused. "Nothing in my actions could have given you reason to suspect I had any intentions of offering for you, if that is what you are implying. I'm sorry if I gave you false hope."

"A kiss is nothing?" Edith asked incredulously. "Do you regularly offer kisses to the females you know?"

"That was a moment of... a mistake after a difficult day for us all," Ralph said cruelly.

Edith sucked in her breath. If he'd struck her she couldn't have felt any worse. "I see. A mistake. Yes, I suppose it was. A mistake on both our parts."

"I'm sorry to have upset you, but I'm always very clear in my intentions. I accept that by kissing you, I overstepped the mark. I assure you, I don't always act like that," Ralph said stiffly. His hands had clenched at his sides when he'd seen the impact his words had on Edith. He'd wanted to enfold her in his arms, but he couldn't.

"But the letters hinted at something else. Some deeper connection between us," Edith said, taking a risk.

There was a stillness for a few moments. Edith half wished she'd held her tongue, but he needed to be completely honest with her. His actions and words were so contradictory, she had no idea who the real man was anymore.

"How did you guess?" Ralph eventually asked gruffly, his own colour heightened.

"I didn't really. I guessed wrong initially, but I always hoped. It wasn't until the last letter that there were just too many coincidences to ignore the connection to you," Edith admitted.

"I shouldn't have sent them."

"I'm glad you did. Without them I'd have just put you down as a rude, arrogant cad."

Ralph spluttered. "By gad! Don't hold your opinion back, Lady Edith. Say whatever you feel."

Edith smiled tentatively. "Even now, I can't do that for fear of more rejection. You say your actions are a mistake, but your words would suggest that they aren't."

Blowing out a breath, Ralph walked across the room, putting more distance between himself and Edith. "It's complicated."

"Life usually is," Edith shrugged.

From outside a sound cracked which made them both start. "What was that?" Edith asked.

"A gunshot, by the sounds of it," Ralph answered. "Strange at this time of night. Unless one of the farmers is shooting at a fox."

It seemed to take only a moment before loud shouting and running in the main areas of the inn brought them both to action.

"Miles!" Edith exclaimed, running towards the door.

"Edith! Stay here!" Ralph commanded, grabbing hold of her around the waist before she reached the door.

"But Miles!" she protested, wriggling against Ralph in order to be free.

"I will check on him. We don't know what's out there yet. Promise me you'll remain here," Ralph commanded.

"But—,"

"Please. I've got to know you're safe."

Edith nodded and stopped her struggle. Ralph seemed to assess whether or not he was being duped but decided she was willing to go along with his request. He left the room at speed, while Edith waited near the now open door.

One gunshot in the night didn't mean that anything was wrong with Miles, but she wouldn't be happy until she saw that her brother was well.

Staff and customers had run out of the inn to see what had occurred, but it wasn't very long before a loud murmuring of many voices approached the inn. Edith was tempted to go to the main doorway of the building, but she couldn't go against her promise to Ralph. She remained at the parlour doorway in an effort to find out what was going on.

The colour drained from her face as she saw the unconscious figure of her brother being carried into the inn by three men. Ralph was giving instructions and Miles was quickly taken upstairs.

Edith had sagged against the doorframe, needing the support of the centuries-old wooden structure. Ralph approached her and gently took her into his arms.

"Come. We've sent for the doctor. There are two wounds but I don't think either are life-threatening. He was just overcome because he was moved," he said gently.

Haunted eyes sought out Ralph's. "What happened?" Edith whispered.

"An unfortunate encounter with a footpad," Ralph explained. "The thief must have just been passing through, but Miles tackled him and he's been caught. He'll swing on the gallows for this."

"I need to go to my brother," Edith said, trying to move, but her legs were unable to support her and she stumbled. Ralph's strong embrace was the only thing which stopped her from dropping to the floor.

"You there, bring some brandy. Now," Ralph commanded a servant and remained supporting Edith until a glass of the amber liquid was brought. "Here. Drink this. You need a little boost," he said gently.

Edith numbly drank the brandy and then returned the empty glass to the servant. "Thank you."

"Ready?" Ralph asked.

"Yes."

Ralph kept his arm around Edith's waist as they walked up the stairs. It was wholly inappropriate, but he was afraid she might falter once more. He hoped Miles' valet had removed most of his master's clothing by the time they reached the bedchamber. There had been a lot of blood, which he didn't want Edith to see. She wouldn't have been able to see much when Miles was brought through the inn as there was so many people around him. In his chamber it would be a different matter.

Ralph was relieved to see that the valet had removed all he could and Miles, although his colouring was grey, looked comfortable in the bed. The room was quite calm after the bustle and noise the incident had caused. Miles' eyes flickered open as they entered the room.

"Oh, Miles!" Edith cried, her voice low. She moved to her brother's side and stroked his face. "What mischief have you been causing?"

"The blasted fellow took me by surprise," he said faintly. "He's a rum padder all right. His mount was impressive. That's what caught my attention in the first instance."

"You and your horseflesh," Edith chided gently.

"The cove wouldn't believe I had no funds on me, the fool. I dragged him off his horse when he wouldn't listen and that's when he shot me," Miles said, the words costing him, as he grimaced and spoke with difficulty.

"You managed to hurt him even though he was armed. He's been restrained and will be locked away for the night. I'll be dealing with him in the morning. He'll either go before the assizes or I'll just send him to London to be tried there," Ralph said grimly, speaking as one of the local magistrates.

"You'd best wait to convict him until you find out if I'll die or not from my wounds," Miles said.

Edith took a sharp intake of breath, but Ralph responded quickly. "He'll swing whatever happens to you. Although, the fact that you're talking in such a way convinces me that you'll soon be up and about. Stop worrying your sister, you buffoon."

Miles glanced at Edith. "Sorry. Black humour is standard military speak."

"How are you feeling?" Edith asked.

"My leg is burning," Miles said, trying to rub his leg to relieve the uncomfortable sensation, whilst at the same time not wanting to touch the bullet hole. "I don't know what happened, but my side is also wounded. There was only one gunshot, so I don't know if I've just fallen and grazed myself."

Both Edith and Ralph could see that the second wound was more serious than a graze, but neither mentioned the fact.

They were soon interrupted by the arrival of the doctor and the pair were ushered out of the room whilst Miles was being examined. Edith protested, but Miles asked her to leave. "I'd rather not cry in front of my sister. Anyway, Pensby here, looks like he could faint at any moment. Take him away, Edith. Please."

Standing outside the now closed bedchamber door, Edith wrapped her arms around her middle. "This is because of my folly. If anything should happen to him…"

Ralph moved over and, without thinking, instinctively wrapped Edith in his arms. Looking into her eyes, he spoke quietly, but firmly. "Don't try take the blame for something you could not have foreseen. This is a safe area, no one would suspect an evening walk would result in an attack."

"But if he should get a fever... My eldest brother Charles caught a chill. Everyone dismissed it as nothing and then the fever started. He raged with delirium for days, until his body became so weak that he couldn't fight any longer. I've only Miles left. Oh, I know I have Mama, but it's not the same. Miles is the last of my siblings. To lose him – I can't. I just can't!" She finished on a choked sob, trying to hold back her tears, but struggling to do so.

Ralph rested his head on her forehead. "I will do anything that is needed to keep him alive. I will spend every last penny if I have to, but don't despair, he is strong. He is in good spirits."

"Charles could speak at first," Edith said dully.

"This is different," Ralph said. He pulled Edith towards him, embracing her fully. She rested her head on his shoulder with a sigh.

"I felt so alone when Papa and my brothers died. It happened that I was the main carer and although I wouldn't have had it any other way, there was no one of whom I could ask advice. Charles and Richard were away from home when Papa was ill. Richard was there when Charles was ill, but he'd gone to pieces. I knew exactly how he felt but I couldn't allow myself to falter."

"You were so brave," Ralph said. "You were very young to have to deal with so much loss. I'm sorry there was no one to support you, but you have an inner strength which obviously helped to get you through it. I admire that and I know your brother does."

"I didn't feel strong or brave at the time," Edith admitted. "I seemed to be a constant watering pot when I went to bed."

"I think I would've been exactly the same. In fact, I'm impressed you managed to keep them contained until you went to bed. I'd probably have cried over everyone," Ralph admitted. He was gratified that his words received a gurgle of appreciation.

"I haven't told anyone about how I felt, not even Miles," Edith admitted quietly. "And I can only do so to you because I'm not looking at you."

Ralph moved, so that he could hold Edith's face in his hands. "You are not alone this time. Your fears aren't foolish, or silly. Look at the way I react with regards to Mother's condition. We respond in the way we do because we care about those we love. You won't receive censure from me for that. But know this, I'm here and I will do anything I can to ease your burden."

"Thank you."

Ralph kissed Edith's forehead and released her as the door opened on Miles' room. The doctor exited, closing the door behind him.

"Your brother has been very fortunate on two accounts, my lady." The doctor started. "The bullet in his leg has travelled straight through without hitting any bone along the way. From what Lord Longdon told me, the gun went off in the struggle the pair were embroiled in."

"What happened to injure the side of his body?" Ralph asked.

"A knife," the doctor responded. "Again, a fortunate hit in the circumstances. It has entered the body, but at the very edge of the torso and not very deeply. I think it was the attacker's last attempt to try and escape. Even with a gunshot wound, Lord Longdon was still putting up a good fight. I have treated the two wounds and bound them, and

I've given him a dose of laudanum because he suffered during the examination."

"What about the risk of fever?" Edith asked.

"There's always a risk, but he is young and healthy, so let's hope not."

"Thank you, Doctor," Ralph said.

"Glad to be of service. I'll call on him tomorrow, unless he does develop a fever. Don't worry if he does," he said noticing the panic on Edith's face. "Just send word and I shall return with haste. I'd advise you both to get some rest, his valet is staying with him for the moment. Our patient won't be stirring tonight with the dose of medication I've given him."

Ralph and Edith entered the bedchamber once the doctor had taken himself downstairs. Miles was fast asleep, looking not quite as grey as he had.

"I'll stay with him," Edith said to the valet.

"No," Ralph said. "You need to rest. Your room is close, I presume?"

"Next door," Edith confirmed.

"Then this capable man can knock on your door if his condition should worsen," Ralph reasoned.

"But—" Edith started.

"If he develops a fever, we will all be required to nurse him. Better to have rest now, because there won't be any time to sleep if he worsens," Ralph argued.

"I suppose so," Edith acknowledged. Turning to the valet, she spoke. "If there is the slightest change..."

"Yes, m'lady, I'll call you immediately. I shan't delay."

"Thank you," Edith responded. She moved to the side of Miles' bed and kissed his cheek before leaving the room with Ralph.

"I could stay here for the night. That way we could both be called if needed," Ralph offered when they were on the landing once more.

"No. You need to check on Lady Pensby," Edith said. "You wouldn't rest easily here not knowing how she is. I have my maid and whilst I have the promise of being called if there is any deterioration, I can retire to my room and remain there."

"Try and get some sleep. I know it won't be easy," Ralph said, taking Edith's arm and walking to the next door along the corridor. "If you need me, send a message and I'll be here within the half hour. Don't hesitate in sending for me."

Edith squeezed Ralph's arm. "You have been so good when you wished to curse me and send me to the devil in a handcart. I am sorry about my apparent disregard for your mother's wellbeing, but I was truly horrified when I saw her here."

"It's done with now," Ralph conceded. "I know how stubborn she can be." Taking her hand, he bent over it, kissing it gently. "Goodnight, Lady Edith. I shall see you very soon."

Chapter 19

Edith entered the private parlour very early the following morning. She sat down not knowing if she could eat any of the food spread out on the side table, but welcomed the warming cup of hot chocolate which was poured for her. Surprised when a maid came through to say Lord Pensby had arrived, she stood to greet him.

"My lord, I didn't expect you at this hour. Please help yourself to some breakfast," Edith said, sitting back at the table in the centre of the room after curtsies and bows had been exchanged.

"I don't make a habit of rising at such an obscenely early hour. I hope Miles appreciates this effort. My valet nearly had apoplexy when I rang for him," Ralph confessed, ordering coffee from the attending maid.

Edith smiled behind her cup. "And how is Lady Pensby?"

"She's surprisingly well. And wanting to come here, only I persuaded her that two invalids would be too much for anyone to deal with. She's asked that I send her a report of Miles as soon as possible," Ralph admitted. It had been a trying conversation as Lady Pensby had insisted that Edith would need her support. Ralph had threatened all sorts of catastrophes if his mother left the house two days in a row.

"Oh dear. She seems as forcefully minded as her son," Edith said quietly.

"I heard that," Ralph said with a grunt. "How is our invalid this morning?"

"Still sleeping when I went to check on him," Edith admitted. "His valet said he'd had a restful night and there are no signs of fever, so far, even without my honey remedy. I shall see how he progresses before I insist on applying it. Miles always hated the smell."

"Yes, he expressed that forcefully enough when you were applying it to my hand."

"He certainly has a way with words."

"I'm glad he had a peaceful night. The doctor was right in that regard, which is something to be positive about," Ralph said thankfully. "And how did you sleep?"

Edith smiled ruefully. "Not as well as Miles, it would appear. But I got some, which is better than nothing."

"Yes, I've learned from experience that one can't be noble when it comes to functioning from too little sleep," Ralph admitted. "I once almost fainted as a result of being pig-headed and refusing to sleep when my mother had taken ill. Thankfully, I have servants who've been employed since before I was born, and they offered some sage advice."

"Yes, old retainers are especially trained to do that," Edith smiled. "It must have been very difficult for you being an only child."

"My mother lives in constant terror that there will come a point in which there is nothing else, other than to have her admitted to the asylum," Ralph admitted to someone outside the inner circle of his family and trusted servants for the first time.

"What? No!" Edith exclaimed. "What does she suffer from which would cause that course of action?"

"It is some sort of spasm, they think caused by a fault in the brain. She can be very ill for days after one comes over her. We've been told that one day, she could experience an attack, I suppose you would call it and it could kill her. She actually fears that less than the asylum, which proves her level of terror at being admitted," Ralph said.

Edith reached out and squeezed Ralph's hand. "I'm so sorry. It must be a constant worry for you. No wonder you are backwards and forwards to your home when visiting London."

"I'd stay at home permanently if I could do as I wished," Ralph confessed. "It is only her determination to send me into society that I go. She frets if she thinks she's restricting my activities, so I give in. When I'm there I keep myself separate most of the time."

"Why? I would think throwing yourself into everything with gusto would take your mind off what's going on back home."

"Because people don't look kindly on a brain illness. It could be something wrong with the bloodline. It could taint future generations," Ralph said with derision. "I'd rather not be whispered about if they decide I've fixed my interest on a young lady."

"I'm presuming you don't know what causes it?"

"No."

"Well how can anyone say for certain that it can infect your descendants? You don't suffer from it," Edith said pragmatically.

Ralph smiled, but there was still derision tinged at the edges. "No. But what they don't understand, they fear. The doctor says that years ago they thought people were possessed by the devil or some form of evil spirits. I would guess some would still suspect the same. Come, enough about my family. Let's go and see how yours is doing."

Miles was still a little groggy because of the laudanum, but awake when his two visitors entered the room. Edith thanked the valet and relieved him of his duties, before turning to Miles and checking his forehead for heat. She breathed a sigh of relief that although a little warm, he didn't seem to be running a fever. She handed a glass of water to him and along with Ralph's help, lifted him into a slight seating position at Miles' request and plumped up his pillows.

"How are you feeling?" she asked.

"Like a cavalry troop has charged right over me," Miles admitted with a wan grin. "Damned inconvenient to be confined to bed."

"I'm just relieved you're not badly hurt. What possessed you to battle with him?" Edith asked.

"He wouldn't believe that I had no blunt on my person and kept pointing his blasted gun at me," Miles explained. "One of us had to bring the situation to a conclusion."

Shaking her head, Edith gently scolded her brother. "You could have been killed."

"Not at all. It was all under control. I did underestimate that he had a knife though. I'll no longer consider footpads as the gentlemen of the road. Damned vagabonds," Miles said with a scowl.

"Your language in front of your sister is appalling," Ralph reprimanded his friend.

"She was brought up with three brothers, she's used to it," Miles shrugged. He turned to Edith. "Anyway, my dear, we can still plan our removal to Barrowfoot in a day or two. The sooner the better, eh? Neither of us will be visiting any balls anytime soon, so we might as well rusticate together."

"I don't think you're ready to move just yet," Ralph said quickly.

"Neither do I. If you think I'm risking you being knocked up on the journey, I'm afraid you're quite mistaken. We'll have to wait here until I have sent mother a letter and she has time to travel to us. She'll want to come immediately," Edith said.

"Do you have to? I'm not in any danger and she will fuss," Miles said, pulling a face.

"You really are a poor son," Ralph said.

"When you've had an hour of mother fussing around you, you realise it's not something you wish to repeat," Miles grimaced.

"You had been away for years, she was pleased to see you," Edith defended her parent.

"But she cried for a whole hour. On my best uniform as well. It took an age for the thing to dry out. Could have stretched it out of shape."

"You do exaggerate," Edith scolded. "But I must write to her and let her know. It's unfair to keep it a secret."

"Give me a couple of days reprieve," Miles begged. "Please."

"Oh, very well, as long as you make no attempt to leave here. We are staying until the doctor says you are fit to travel," Edith said firmly.

"Yes, ma'am," Miles responded with a grin.

"How do you put up with him?" Ralph asked with a smirk.

"With great fortitude and plenty of brandy," Edith replied without hesitation.

"Longdon, you have a sister who's an old soak," Ralph said, to a harrumph from Edith.

*

Ralph left Edith for the afternoon to check on his mother but returned in the evening. She was in the private parlour when Ralph entered the room.

"Have you deserted your brother already? I wouldn't blame you if you had," Ralph said pleasantly.

"No. He said he wanted to use his valet's services to wash and get changed. He's going to be a difficult patient," Edith admitted.

"I can sit and play cards with him for a while, if that would help," Ralph offered.

"Would you? Oh, thank you. I know it's through boredom that he's fretting, he isn't normally still for so long," Edith explained.

"I can understand that. I think I've trained myself to be more patient. It helps when sitting for hours in the same room and watching for any sign of recovery," Ralph admitted.

"If you are free tomorrow and have no objection – I wouldn't like it to cause any upset or – but I would like to visit with your mother – for the shortest time and only if she is well enough – I just thought whilst I was still here –," Edith babbled before running out of steam.

Ralph smiled, shaking his head. "How could I refuse such an eloquent request?"

"Beast!" Edith answered.

"Most certainly. I actually can't refuse because my mother has informed me that if I didn't issue an invitation to you, she would set out once more to visit here. She's very worried about Longdon and has suggested you both come to stay with us," Ralph repeated the invitation, which hid the long discussion which had gone on before an agreement was reached between mother and son.

"Oh no! I wouldn't cause any work or put either of you to any trouble. We are comfortable here and at least I have your permission to visit her. That is enough," Edith said quickly.

"You make me sound like I'm her goaler," Ralph said.

Edith smiled. "You worry about her. I understand that. Any other reference is down to your own paranoia, my lord."

"Now, who's being the beast?" Ralph asked, standing. "I shall leave you be, Lady Edith. I have to take my chance and fleece your brother whilst he is in a weakened state."

"As he has told me of your prowess at the gaming tables, and you have admitted the same to some extent, I know he isn't foolish enough to pit his wits against you normally," Edith said, falsely prim.

"Even more reason to take my chance while I can," Ralph said before bowing and leaving Edith alone.

She sighed when the door closed. Being in such a close proximity to the man she was in love with was torture. Last night, he'd been supportive and decisive when she'd been thrown into turmoil because of the fear of losing Miles nearly overwhelming her. Now, she was back to her normal, practical self. Last night, she could have equalled her mother with the level of dramatics that had threatened to overtake her. Ralph's calm reactions had helped to soothe her panicked state and she would be ever thankful to him for that.

Now, this more easy-going, teasing nature was sweet agony. He'd been clear in his rejection of becoming involved with anyone. It didn't stop her heart from hoping or looking for every slight word or look which could be interpreted as something which was exclusively for her. That he would be a gentleman to anyone in difficulty, she knew, even without proof of his actions. Her heart was just struggling to accept the fact that it wasn't for her specifically he was motivated to act.

She was glad to be leaving the inn for an hour or two the following morning. Hopefully, it would help to clear her head a little.

*

The day started with a crisp, bright morning. Edith took a lungful of the fresh air before stepping into the carriage, she didn't miss the air in London one little bit. Ralph had arrived and although she'd fussed over Miles for the few hours they were alone, he was well and sitting up in bed. It meant she could leave him with a clear conscience.

Being taken to Ralph's home with his blessing, was a strange feeling. She'd assured him she wouldn't stay too long, not wishing for the understanding they shared to be spoiled. Being driven through the fringes of the village and into the parkland of Lymewood, Edith refused to let herself dwell on what might be. Ralph had shown no indication that he was doing anything but helping Miles in his time of need.

Lady Pensby greeted Edith as if she hadn't seen her for months and after fussing over her to be seated, take tea, and choose far too many cakes, the ladies finally settled.

"Tell me all of what has happened. I know Ralph won't have told me everything, boys never do," Lady Pensby said, pouring tea.

Edith told her briefly of what had happened. "Miles is surprisingly well considering what his injuries are. He tells me it isn't the first time he's been hurt, which I have to admit to being shocked at hearing because his letters never hinted at him being wounded. I've questioned him about it, but he just laughed it off saying, it's done with now, no use going over old war stories. Which actually worries me even more." Edith was now wholly convinced that her brother was hiding much from his family about his experiences. She felt sorry that he couldn't confide in her and hoped that he trusted someone enough to speak about it.

"I suppose he didn't want to make his family even more anxious than you would have already been. It's admirable that he wanted to protect you."

"He said Father had died and Charles was ill, so he wasn't going to add to the distress already being felt at home," Edith said. "I feel we let him down in some ways, by not supporting him when he probably needed it more than any of us."

"I doubt he would agree with you. Ralph tells me your brother speaks highly of how you dealt with the troubles you faced. You were so young to go through so much," Lady Pensby said sympathetically.

"It was hard," Edith admitted. "But I suppose during the day, I just had to get on with things. My mother has never been of a strong constitution when it comes to dealing with any trying situation, but especially family troubles, so I had to take the burden from her as much as I could."

"She was very lucky to have you. I'd certainly want you by my side in a crisis."

"Oh, I think your confidence would be misplaced," Edith said quickly. "If it hadn't been for Lord Pensby when Miles was shot, I'd have crumbled. He was the one who took control, for which I'll be eternally grateful."

"He's very good," Lady Pensby agreed.

Edith flushed a little. "He has helped to entertain Miles these last two days. Miles soon gets restless. To have someone there who isn't afraid to curse my brother when he mentions leaving his chamber is a help. If I do it, I can be accused of being a meddling sister, but he wouldn't accuse Lord Pensby of the same."

"I think Ralph has other motivations, as well as aiding his friend," Lady Pensby said gently.

"Oh?"

"If my son hasn't already fallen in love with you, I'm not his mother. Whenever he mentions you his whole demeanour changes. I like the way that talking about you makes his eyes sparkle and his mouth twitch when he is recounting what mischief you've got up to. No one else has ever had that effect on him."

Edith smiled, but her cheeks burned. "To be fair, Lady Pensby, he doesn't spend much time in company. There are far prettier young ladies out there than I; I wouldn't put any store against his reaction."

"It's not all about the way we look, although I might have to reassess my opinion of you being a sensible girl if you continue to come out with such nonsense. You are very pretty, my child," Lady Pensby responded. "There has to be a spark of attraction, but thankfully, it's more than that. You challenge him and make him laugh. Those are excellent qualities, especially when dealing with someone as bloody-minded as Ralph."

"You are a mother who knows her own son well, I see," Edith said, laughing.

"Oh yes. What I need from you is a plan as to how we can get him to realise just what a treasure you are and propose to you," Lady Pensby said, even more convinced that Edith would be perfect as a daughter-in-law.

Edith looked uncomfortable and glanced away, avoiding Lady Pensby's gaze.

"What is it, my dear? Have my words upset you? Have you a beau already?" the older woman asked.

"No!" Edith said, glancing up. "It's just that when you speak of interfering with Lord Pensby and persuading him to marry – my mother made my coming out far less pleasurable than it should have been. Our conversation reminded me of her actions a little."

"In what way?"

"Whenever I spoke to a gentleman, she wanted to know all the details about him. She tried at every opportunity to promote me to anyone who was pleasant to me. They didn't even need to have shown any marked preference. Politeness was interpreted as interest in Mother's mind and she would, quite embarrassingly, openly make it obvious that I would welcome a proposal. I've seen enough horrified expressions from even the most elderly gentlemen to last me a lifetime," Edith explained.

"Oh dear, you poor thing. That must have been horrendous to have to go through that, especially so publicly."

"I want it to be a joint decision when I marry. For the man who I care for to want to marry me for who I am, not because we have been pushed together because of circumstance, or our parents. I don't wish to upset my mother, or you, but I can't live my life to anyone's wishes other than my own. I realise that makes me sound a selfish chit, but I hope you understand my meaning," Edith explained.

"You don't have a *tendre* for my son. I am so sorry for babbling on in such a way. I realise a mother sees the best in her children and I apologise that I've caused you discomfort," Lady Pensby said in earnest.

"Oh, it's not that!" Edith said quickly. "Your son is everything anyone could wish for. I just can't agree with schemes and plans, especially as he's professed no wish to marry."

Lady Pensby looked at Edith with an inscrutable expression. "When did he say that?"

"Oh, some time ago," Edith admitted. "Please don't tell him I've mentioned it. I can't imagine he would be happy at us talking about him in such a personal way."

"I imagine he would have expected it," Lady Pensby said with a smile. "Don't worry though, whatever we've said is between us. I won't be mentioning any particulars to Ralph." Although I will be finding out more from him, she thought to herself.

"Thank you. And now it is time I returned to Miles," Edith said, knowing there would be no argument from her hostess about staying if she used her brother as the excuse for leaving.

"I do hope you can visit me tomorrow," Lady Pensby said. "I have truly enjoyed your company."

"As have I. I promise I will try my best," Edith responded before taking her leave.

Chapter 20

Lady Pensby had retired to her chamber when her son returned home. As he always did, he visited her before anything else took his attention, concern for her came above all other demands on his time.

"How are you?" he asked, crossing to the bed and kissing her cheek.

"Tired, but glad I received a visit. I like Lady Edith."

"That's because she's on her best behaviour with you," Ralph said dryly.

Lady Pensby smiled. "She mentioned a little about her mother. She seems to be one of those women who is overly dependent on her family's support and cosseting," she said gently, feeling her way into the conversation she wished to have.

"Dreadful woman," Ralph said without hesitation.

"She sounds like the type of woman to encourage unsuitable matches, just to be rid of her children and to be able to crow to others that her offspring are married."

"Yes. I think Sage wouldn't have got as close to the family as he did if it hadn't been for the mother. She nearly helped deliver her daughter to a cad. Miles said he'd had to give his mother a dressing down after she'd torn a strip off Lady Edith for refusing Sage. It wouldn't have been a happy match, even I could see that," Ralph said, some of his inner feelings showing in his expression.

"I would imagine Lady Edith requiring someone who could challenge her, as well as indulge her after all she's been through these last few years. I do hope she finds a suitable match," Lady Pensby said airily.

"Mother," Ralph warned.

"Oh, don't look at me with such daggers! I didn't mean you," Lady Pensby countered.

"Good."

"You don't deserve someone like Lady Edith."

"I beg your pardon?" Ralph spluttered.

"She deserves someone who wants her above everything else. You'll marry some poor sap who'll be afraid of you when you finally accept it's time to continue the family name. That will not be for years to come, so I've no plans to pair you up with Lady Edith, I assure you," Lady Pensby explained.

"Good grief, you make me sound a callow fellow!" Ralph said. "Your opinion of me could be worse, but it would be a struggle to see how, I think."

"What? Have I misunderstood your feelings about the matrimonial state?" Lady Pensby asked, all mock wide-eyed-innocence.

Ralph narrowed his eyes at his mother. "You know full well I don't want to marry. Ever. Continuing the title for future generations would be my only motivation."

"I can't understand why, though," Lady Pensby said honestly. "It's a sad way to view the future. Alone, which you will be, even in a marriage of convenience."

Ralph sighed and walked to the window. He looked blindly outside for a few moments before turning to his mother. "When I say what I have to say, I want no arguments, no discussions."

"That's a little unfair."

"It's the way it has to be. If you want my honesty, I don't want you to attempt an argument against what I've decided. You have to respect my decisions as your son and the head of the family."

"I can see I'm not going to like this," Lady Pensby said, folding her arms in anticipation.

"I have no wish to marry at the moment," Ralph started, pushing aside the inner feeling of heaviness when he uttered those words. If his mind wandered to picture Edith's face, he shook it away and continued. "I refuse to put you at risk in any way and that includes introducing new people, new stresses on you. I want to keep you with me as long as I can and I will do everything in my power to ensure that is the case. You will never move to the Dower House, you will remain here where you can have the best care."

"Oh, Ralph. My sickness is not a reason to stop yourself being happily married," Lady Pensby said.

"I am happy. I have you and that's all I need," Ralph said, remaining at the window. He felt exposed and a little raw at voicing the words which would keep him from the life partner he would have wished to have had his circumstances been different.

"Oh, my poor boy, you are so wrong, but I see what it is costing you to speak so, so I won't push you on it," Lady Pensby said gently.

"Thank you," Ralph said. "Please, let's not mention it again. It's been said and there is no need to go over it now, or in the future. Now I'll leave you to rest. You've had a busy day."

*

Edith almost barrelled into Ralph when he entered the parlour the following morning. "How is your mother?" she demanded.

Ralph had sent a note over to explain that Edith shouldn't expect to visit that day due to Lady Pensby feeling exhausted. "She's resting. The doctor has visited and increased the dosage of the new drugs he is trying, so she's sleeping. He's said that is to be expected as a perfectly normal result, so I took the opportunity to look in on Miles before sitting with her."

"It was my visits, wasn't it?" Edith asked, still mortified at the realisation.

"It will have put a strain on her, yes," Ralph admitted. "As will a talk I had with her last night. Don't trouble yourself though, last week I would have been angry at the thought of exertion causing her weakness, but not anymore. I had a long, hard look at her life after I'd spoken to her yesterday."

"What's changed?"

"Speaking to Miles, actually. He explained about the way he looks at life since his return from war and it made me look at my mother's way of life," Ralph said. "I realised that keeping her separate from everything means that she isn't living, it is just an existence. If she lives a shorter life but that life is happier, then hers will have been a good life. I was being selfish in trying to keep her alive longer because I want her to live at any cost. For that cost to be her enjoyment of life is too high, so I won't be so draconian in future." He didn't mention that he couldn't change so much as to bring a wife and children into his home, for that would be too much for her to deal with.

Edith crossed to Ralph and put her arm through his. Resting her head on his shoulder for a moment in a show of sympathy and understanding, she pulled away. "No wonder your mother adores you, you really do have her best interests at heart. I completely withdraw any reference to a gaoler I've made in the past."

"I suppose that's something," Ralph said, his mouth twitching slightly. "I shall pop in to see your brother before I return home. Do you join me?"

"No. I'll stay here," Edith said. "I'll not crowd you both whilst you exchange insults."

"You are quite able to fight your own corner in that regard," Ralph said with approval.

"Yes, but sometimes it's nice to pretend I'm a true lady of quality," Edith said primly.

"A deluded one," Ralph said as he left the room to Edith's laugh.

*

Edith entered Miles' chamber long after Ralph had visited his friend. She was not surprised that her brother was seated in front of the fire, fully dressed, except for his frock coat.

"You're looking well," she said, sitting in the opposite seat to her brother.

"Yes. The only sickness I suffer from now is that I'm sick of kicking my heels here," Miles admitted. "I think we should leave tomorrow."

"Oh."

"I'm well enough to travel," Miles insisted.

"Well enough for a letter to be sent to mother?" Edith teased.

"You are the worst sister sometimes," Miles grimaced. "Could we not just pretend it didn't happen?"

"And the hanging of a highwayman who attacked a cavalryman won't be reported widely in the newspapers when it comes to court?" Edith asked.

"Good point. Damn it!" Miles cursed. "We'll set off as planned and send the letter at the same time. She can travel home if she wishes or stay in London with her coven of witches."

"That's so ungentlemanly."

"You sound just like Pensby. Talking of whom—"

"Which we weren't," Edith interrupted.

"Talking of Pensby," Miles continued with a raised eyebrow. "I'm presuming you are still mooning over him?"

"Oh, that your wounds would have taught you some delicacy," Edith said.

"How the devil would getting shot teach me delicacy?" Miles asked, dumbfounded.

"You were shot because you insisted on arguing and fighting when an apology and reasoning would have been more appropriate," Edith said, trying to ignore the fact her brother was staring at her as if she'd gone mad.

"I'd rather dance with the devil than apologise to a damned cur!" Miles ground out. "Are you out of your senses, Edith? Is this what being smitten does to one? I'll be sure to avoid it, if it is."

"I am not smitten!" Edith defended herself.

"I see the way you gaze at him," Miles shrugged. "I also see the way he looks at you."

"For all the good it does either of us," Edith responded.

"He's not the marrying kind."

"I know. I know. There's no need to go on."

"I wasn't," Miles said. "Come, Edith, I don't think he would make you happy. Do you?"

"I'd like to think I'd be the better judge of what would make me happy, rather than you. But I don't want to argue, so we shall change the subject," Edith said. "There is no point in going over old ground. I tried and my foolish scheme failed. I'm astute enough to accept defeat when it stares me in the face."

"I'm sorry," Miles said, his tone gentle. "I would welcome him into the family if he was the one who you chose. I say that you wouldn't suit not because I dislike him, just that he has never mentioned marrying for love, but you have. If he was of the same mind, we wouldn't be having this conversation. I feel it's time to let go your hopes with regards to him."

"I know. I will. I would like to call in and see Lady Pensby before we leave the area though. I promise it isn't anything to do with Lord Pensby. I really like her and would hate just to send a note, rather than take my leave of her. Perhaps we could do it on our way through?" Edith asked.

"If you're sure it's not a bad idea," Miles said unconvinced.

"I'm sure."

Chapter 21

Lady Pensby greeted the brother and sister as if they were long lost friends. She was seated in the bright, large drawing room which Edith had admired on her first visit to Lymewood.

Passing tea around, Edith smiled at Lady Pensby as she questioned Miles about his career and travels.

Ralph accepted the cup offered to him by Edith and smiled up at her. "My mother has finished her interrogation of you it would seem. Now she has moved on to your brother. I worry his weakened state will prevent him from putting up much resistance."

"Yes, if Wellington had known of her existence, he could have used her for any prisoners they took. All Napoleon's secrets would have been quickly revealed," Edith said, sitting herself on a chair next to Ralph. "She's looking very well."

"Yes, the increase in medication seems to have settled everything down again," Ralph said with relief. "I long for the concoction the doctor has sent for to arrive and we can start to try that. The doctor assures us it has some good results, but it's taking forever to reach these shores."

"It must be hard on you both, never knowing when to expect the worst," Edith sympathised.

"I suppose after a while, it becomes almost normal," Ralph admitted. "Through necessity we've both become isolated, but especially Mother. She will miss you even though your acquaintance has been very recent."

"I will miss her too," Edith replied honestly. "I'm glad I have the opportunity to speak to you before we leave. I wanted to ask you something about the letters."

Ralph flushed and looked warily in Miles' direction.

"He doesn't know that you have written," Edith said. "No one does. I have to ask if you knew it was me you were writing to?"

Looking uncomfortable, Ralph nodded slightly. "Yes. I did."

"How? I never told a soul until I received the first of your letters. Was it when Mama brought in that blasted parcel?" Edith asked, her cheeks still flushing with colour at the thought of that embarrassing experience.

"No. I knew prior to that," Ralph admitted.

"How?" Edith pushed. "I must know the truth of the matter for it has puzzled me since I thought the writer knew who I was."

Ralph sighed. "Please don't criticise him for doing so, but your brother told me of your scheme."

"Miles?" Edith gasped.

"Shh. You don't want to let him know we have been corresponding, do you?" Ralph hissed at her.

"I-no. I don't. But why would he tell you?" Edith asked, anger bubbling.

"He was worried about his sister. At that time I hadn't been reacquainted with you, so I seemed like the perfect person to confide in," Ralph shrugged. "I would never have told anyone else."

"No. And neither should my brother," Edith hissed.

"Sometimes we need someone to talk to," Ralph admitted for the first time. "Miles needed me and I needed you."

Edith was silent for a little while, trying to process what she'd heard and the implications of Ralph's words. Eventually, she turned to look him fully in the eye. "You used me."

"What? No! I turned to you in my hour of need," Ralph said quickly.

"You knew from the start that I was looking for someone to love and yet you wrote me such words," Edith said.

"I told you in the first letter that I wasn't interested in marriage," Ralph defended himself.

"Yet, your words were more than those of a friend. Especially after our ball. You sent a letter to expressly tell me that you thought I was beautiful. Why would you do that?"

Ralph dragged his hand through his hair in frustration. "You'd had a bad night, when it should have been your finest hour; the darling of the ball. Instead that cad upset you. I just wanted you to know that you looked magnificent. It was the truth, not false flattery," Ralph said in frustration.

Edith glared at him. "You've been worse than Mr Sage."

"How dare you compare me to that sly cheater!" Ralph almost exploded, vainly trying to keep his voice low.

"He didn't try to bamboozle me. His actions from the start were that of a fortune hunter – shallow flattery and obsequious attentions. I saw what he was about and it didn't fool me, or concern me, I was never going to develop any feelings for him," Edith snapped. "You filled my days with your charm, wit and intelligence and filled my nights with your written words. It meant I completely and utterly fell in love with you whilst you were purely toying with me."

"I wasn't doing anything of the sort," Ralph snapped in return, guilt at the words he'd heard making him respond harshly. "I was very clear with my intent, both by verbally expressing my feelings and putting it in writing that I wasn't looking for a wife!"

"Yet, your actions showed otherwise. You were inconsistent at best and damned misleading at worst! I need to leave," Edith stood on unsteady legs, which faltered even more when she turned to see the stunned expressions on both her brother and Lady Pensby's faces. "Miles. We need to go home."

"Yes, I think we do," Miles said stiffly, glaring at Ralph. "My lady, please excuse us," he said bowing slightly to Lady Pensby.

"Oh, don't go like this," Lady Pensby said quickly. "Stay and talk this through."

"I think enough has been said," Edith said. "I'm sorry to leave on such a sour note, but please forgive me. I need to go."

"Please write and let me know you arrive home safely," Lady Pensby begged. She received a reassuring nod from Edith.

"Pensby, I have much to say to you, but doubt I'll get the chance to do so anytime soon. Know this, it's a good thing I'm injured, or you'd receive the thrashing of your life," Miles ground out as he passed his friend. "I don't know what game you were playing but you are a damned cur for taking the information I gave you in confidence and using it for your own advantage!"

Ralph didn't utter a word in retaliation, just watching as the brother and sister walked out of his drawing room. The room was filled with silence until they heard the sound of the carriage wheels crunching on the gravel of the drive. When the sound eventually faded, Lady Pensby spoke.

"I am too exhausted and upset to request an explanation about all that has gone on, but I shall insist on knowing the full story at a later time."

"Are you feeling ill?" Ralph asked, immediately alert to his mother's needs.

"For once I wish you would reflect on your own behaviour, rather than focusing on my needs," Lady Pensby said tartly. "I never thought I'd be ashamed of you, Ralph, but at the moment I'm struggling to defend what I heard. I shall leave you for the time being. I need to be quiet."

Ralph was left, his ears stinging from his mother's rebuke and his heart heavy from the expression on Edith's face. He'd never felt as lost in his life and it was his own foolish fault.

*

For the first few miles, neither brother nor sister spoke. Each was wrapped up in their own thoughts and unwilling to start the conversation which needed to be had. The air was thick with unhappiness and confusion.

Eventually, Miles broke the silence. "How long have you been corresponding with Pensby?"

Edith had been angry, but now she just felt weary. She wanted anything rather than to go over the subject of her folly with Miles, but she owed him an explanation. "After I'd cancelled the advertisement, I received one last letter. It seemed to come from someone who was suffering from deep sadness rather than someone intent on a flirtation. He did state that he wasn't interested in marriage, but of course after the first letter, I persuaded myself that he favoured me and didn't mean what he'd said."

"How many letters have there been?" Miles asked.

"Not many. Although, enough for me to think I'd found my ideal man," Edith all but snorted.

"Did you know it was Pensby?"

"No. I hoped it was him if I'm being honest, but for a while, I actually thought it was Mr Sage. He signed the letter Mr S, you see. I jumped to conclusions, which were the wrong ones to start with," Edith admitted.

Miles frowned for a moment or two. "Swanson. The family name is Swanson, so technically Pensby is Mr S."

"I didn't know that. I suppose I should have done," Edith said, feeling even more of a fool. "I was so relieved when I discovered it wasn't Mr Sage. I only found out in the carriage when he was trying to abduct me. I couldn't understand how his words and actions could be so different. It was such a relief to find out I'd been wrong in my assumptions in that regard at least."

"You were so determined to make contact with Pensby the following morning. Had you guessed again about the writer?" Miles asked.

"He'd sent what was to be his last letter, but some of the clues in it led me to be convinced that it was him who'd written the letters. When it was confirmed that he'd gone out of town, I was sure I had discovered the true writer and had to follow him. You see, I'd been stupid in both respects," Edith said.

"I don't understand."

"I'd fallen in love with the writer of the letters and Lord Pensby. I hoped for them to be the same person, because I didn't know what I'd do if they weren't. What I foolishly admitted in the drawing room was true. I've been smitten with him for weeks now. That makes me a bigger fool, I know" Edith said darkly.

"I did warn you away from him," Miles responded. "I tried to put the thought in your mind that he wouldn't come up to snuff."

"I know. Unfortunately, my head might have listened, but my heart didn't," Edith admitted. "I didn't set out to fall in love with a man who doesn't want to marry, I can assure you."

"No. I suppose not. If it helps, I do think he has feelings for you," Miles said trying to console Edith.

"It doesn't help actually. Especially as I'm travelling away from him at a high speed, having confessed my feelings to him. There is no sound of hooves behind us, trying to stop the carriage and declare he has been mistaken and he can't live without me after all. Somehow knowing that he liked me doesn't help with the self-loathing I'm struggling with at the moment," Edith said tartly.

"I suppose it wouldn't," Miles responded grimly. "I could have swung for him when I realised what he'd done."

"That wouldn't achieve anything. I'm just glad I'd already left London before finding out. This way, at least I don't have to confess that I've been a complete fool to Susan."

"What has Miss King got to do with it?" Miles asked.

"Nothing as such. But as best friends, we confide in each other, so she knows about the letters and my feelings," Edith admitted.

"Oh," Miles responded.

"I hope you intend to keep this pace going on our journey, brother, because the more distance I can put between myself and Lord Pensby, the better," Edith said, turning her head away from Miles and blindly looking out of the window.

She would never forget Ralph's shocked expression when she'd confessed she loved him, or cease to burn with shame every time she thought about it.

Chapter 22

Lady Pensby had eaten in her room and slept for most of the evening. Ralph had checked on her, but she'd been asleep, so he hadn't disturbed her, leaving her nurse to watch over his mother. Although he knew they would have a conversation about Edith, he was glad to put it off for as long as possible. He'd done everything wrong and the less he thought about it the better.

A pity then, that he could think of little else.

Early the following morning, he rode out on his horse, as far away as he could from houses, farms and especially people. He'd always been seen as a more taciturn person, but today if he had the misfortune to meet anyone along his way, they would probably put his main characteristic as downright miserable.

A virtually sleepless night had done nothing to clear his head and when he'd been fortunate enough to doze off, his dreams had been filled with images of Edith's disappointed face. It hadn't led to a refreshing night's rest, hence his early exploration of his wider parkland.

Eventually, he couldn't prolong his return any further, the need to check on his mother greater than his wish to escape. He allowed his horse to head for the stables. The grooms receiving nothing but a nod when they took the reins, decided today was not the day to try and banter with their master and quietly got on with their work.

Entering the hallway, Ralph discarded his hat and gloves. "Where is my mother?" he asked the butler.

"In her sitting room," the butler responded.

"I shall get changed and visit her there. Please serve tea in half an hour," Ralph instructed.

"Yes. m'lud."

It wasn't long before Ralph entered his mother's sitting room, fixing his cuffs as he walked into the room.

"Good morning, dearest. Did you sleep well?" he asked, going as he always did to give her a kiss.

"I slept better than you from the looks of it," Lady Pensby responded, offering her cheek to her son.

Ralph grimaced. "I'd hoped the horse ride would hide some of the evidence."

"I think the rings under your eyes will take more than that to fade."

"Wonderful."

Lady Pensby lapsed into silence, watching Ralph. They hadn't spoken by the time the tea tray was brought in. Ralph busied himself with dealing with the tea, prolonging the need for the dreaded conversation to start.

When he'd handed his mother a cup he sat on the seat next to her. He couldn't face any tea himself at that moment. "I'm sorry you had to witness what you did."

"I'm sorry my son inflicted such pain on a young woman who didn't deserve it," Lady Pensby said quietly.

"You've always been able to get right to the crux of the matter haven't you?" Ralph replied, leaning forward and rubbing his hands over his face. "Would it help to know that I honestly didn't mean to hurt her?"

"I've already given you credit for that," Lady Pensby admitted.

"Unfortunately, that doesn't make me feel any better."

"Did you not suspect how she felt about you? Surely there must have been signs?"

"Certainly not after our first meeting," Ralph said. "We argued."

"Always a good start to a romance," Lady Pensby smiled slightly.

"Afterwards, there was some attraction between us, yes, I think so," Ralph said. "We certainly sought each other out. And how could anyone blame me? She's witty, considerate, welcoming and beautiful. She takes my breath away she's so beguiling."

"She doesn't consider herself so," Lady Pensby said. "She confessed it here and it wasn't false modesty. I genuinely think she doesn't see herself to be anything out of the ordinary."

Ralph had looked at his mother in disbelief, but then shook his head. "It's just like her. To be fair though, I don't think her family see her as such either. In a conversation before I was reacquainted with her, Miles expressed his concern that she was already on the shelf. He said that she had little to offer a man anything other than her fortune. I thought he was being harsh, but when I met her, I was convinced he was a fool."

"Why did you start writing to her?"

"Ah, that's the difficult part," Ralph started. "I don't really know."

"Was it to confess feelings that you couldn't declare face to face?"

"In a way, I suppose, but they weren't feelings of love, before you accuse me of that. It was other issues," Ralph answered.

"The pressures you have day-to-day with a life that isn't how you'd choose it to be?" Lady Pensby said gently, resting her hand on her son's arm when he stiffened and looked at her alarmingly. "I'm your mother. I've known and watched you almost every day of your life. Of course I know some of the struggles you so admirably try to keep from everyone."

"I like my life as it is," Ralph defended himself.

"But it could be better."

"When you are well, or stable, then life will be better. That will be more than enough to make me content."

"Oh, my dear boy. It isn't how you should be spending your life," Lady Pensby said sadly.

"I'm with you. I want nothing else."

"I thought you never lied to me."

"I'm not," Ralph flushed.

Lady Pensby laughed. "You are a poor liar. Now, I have a few things I want to make clear."

"I don't like the sound of this."

"Probably not, but I've tried to say it before and you've ignored me. This time you'd better listen," Lady Pensby warned.

"Go on." Ralph resigned himself to a lecture, the substance of which he wasn't going to agree with.

"Unless you go after that girl and persuade her to marry you, I'm going to take myself off to the asylum," Lady Pensby said firmly.

"You'll do nothing of the sort!" Ralph exploded.

"Oh, yes I will. If my staying here is going to prevent you living your life as it should, then I would willingly, yes willingly, admit myself to that place."

"You wouldn't."

"Do you want to test me, Ralph? Really?" Lady Pensby asked.

Ralph stood and walked across the room to stand at the fireplace. He got hold of the brass poker and took his initial frustration out on the carefully stacked logs of the fire. When he'd contented himself by sending sparks flying up the chimney and caused the logs to hiss due to their rough treatment, he hung the poker back on its stand.

"It's not as simple as you think," he said, turning to his mother.

"I'm dying to find out why not."

"I refuse to upset your health by you moving to the Dower House and being away from all that is familiar and safe," Ralph admitted. "Nothing or no one is worth that disruption and the consequences it could cause."

"You do realise how close the Dower House is to the main building, don't you?" Lady Pensby asked with an amused smile.

"It's not just about the location. It's about the staff, the routine, and the accommodation," Ralph answered gruffly.

"Those all can be overcome. Easily," Lady Pensby insisted. "And I have to admit moving to the house, which was always going to be my home eventually, is far preferable than the asylum."

"I suppose that's something," came the sarcastic reply. "Remaining under this roof is even better."

"I don't think it is," Lady Pensby said gently. "I've worried about whether or not you were being noble when you'd never married. To discover that is exactly what you're trying to be, convinces me even more that there needs to be some separation between our lives."

"No! I want to spend as much time with you as I can. I accept that you should do more than you have been doing. I realise you weren't living a full life, but to change completely that would be too much. I can't risk losing you. I can't," Ralph said desperately.

"Come here, my foolish boy," his mother said, holding out her hands to her son. Ralph went across and crouched on the floor in front of her. He rested his head on her lap as he'd done when a young boy. She stroked his hair gently. "I want to spend time with you, but the thing I want most in the world is to see you settled and happy. Whether or not I had this illness, I could die today, tomorrow, or in ten years' time. No one knows. Just as we didn't know when your father would die."

"I don't want to do anything to risk extra strain on you. A wife and children would do that," Ralph said quietly.

"I lived with you as a child."

"But we had a quiet life."

"Yes, we did. That was only because I was afraid to leave you whilst you were so young. I don't know if it actually did me any good or not, for the attacks still happened. Now though, I will have peace in the Dower House when I need it. I will visit, or you and your gaggle of children, for I can see you with many, can visit me when I feel up to it. You'll be able to make as much noise as you like when you're here in the main house. Just how a family home should be. This house needs life, Ralph. It has been silent too long."

Ralph closed his eyes and took a steadying breath. "The picture you paint, sounds so idyllic, so reachable."

"That's because it is."

"Yet I've managed to hurt the only person I could create that home with."

"Look at me," Lady Pensby commanded. Ralph sat up, his face clasped in his mother's hands as she looked deep into his eyes. "If she truly loves you, which I think she does, she will forgive you eventually. You'll just have to find a way of convincing her that you're worth the second chance."

"That's all I need to do?" Ralph said with a small smile.

"I'm not saying it will be easy but I'm sure you'll come up with some scheme to persuade her."

"Her brother won't let me within fifty miles of her," Ralph said grimly.

"Well, she fell in love with you through the written word once, you'll just have to make her do it again," came the firm response.

Chapter 23

Edith's hair streamed behind her as her horse leapt over the five-foot fence. She heard the concerned cry from her groom, but ignored it, encouraging her horse to gallop away from the gate as soon as its hooves had touched the ground. Tearing across the field she crouched low over the beast's neck and urged it to jump the hedge.

She whooped, as once more she was airborne, unrestrained and free. A stumble as the front hooves hit the ground made her pull on the reins to bring her favourite steed to a stop.

"Whoa, fella," she said, coming to a standstill.

Swinging herself off the horse, she checked his legs and was dismayed to find his front left leg was sensitive to her touch.

"Oh, you poor boy," she murmured as she stroked the panting beast's muzzle. "Was it a jump too far? We'll get you back home the slow way."

Starting to lead the animal home, her groom was finally able to catch up to her. "You rode him too hard, Lady Edith."

"I know. You don't need to curse me, I'm ashamed I've hurt him. Miles will be furious," Edith admitted.

"You're trying higher hedges every day. The master will string me up if you take a tumble," the groom admitted.

"He won't put any of the blame on you," Edith assured him. "Even he struggles to keep me on the gentler obstacles."

They walked back to Barrowfoot House slowly, so as not to cause further harm to the horse. When they arrived back at the stables, Edith wouldn't leave until the injured leg had been checked by the head groom. He'd shaken his head at Edith in a way that transported her back to her youth, when he would curse her for being reckless with the animals in her need for speed.

Eventually, Edith returned to the house, immediately going upstairs to change. She was too late for lunch, so requested some bread, ham and cheese in the drawing room. Fifteen minutes later, she finally sat down to a warming drink and some sustenance.

She'd only just finished her light meal when Miles burst into the room. Looking up, she braced herself for the inevitable scolding.

"If you're determined to ride neck or nothing over every hedge on the land, be good enough to do it without hurting an innocent beast. He'll be out of action for days, if not longer," Miles snarled.

"I know. I could've cursed myself to the devil, I assure you," Edith admitted. "I shouldn't have done the two in quick succession."

"You shouldn't have done either," Miles snapped. "Don't think your addle-brained riding doesn't get reported back."

Edith scowled. "Is there to be no freedom?"

"Not when you're causing injury to something who doesn't have a say in the matter," Miles said firmly. "I don't know where this crazed death wish has come from, although I can guess, but it has to stop."

"Keep your overactive imagination to yourself," Edith responded tartly. "I ride for nothing other than the thrill of the wind in my face."

"If you say so," Miles said unconvinced. "Whatever the reason, it has to stop."

"I don't normally make a habit of misusing my horses and of course I know it can't continue," Edith said. "Now stop lecturing me. You're sounding like Mother."

"Fortunately for us both, she's having too much fun in London to be bothered about us," Miles said.

"Who would have thought that we'd be hiding out in the countryside and she'd be enjoying the season to the full?" Edith said with a chuckle. "Funny how life turns out."

"I'm improving every day. I'll soon be well enough to stand the journey and activities when I arrive, which means I should return to London," Miles said.

"We knew I was going to spend some time here alone," Edith said. "I think I'm going to write to cousin Adele and see if she would like an extended visit with me. We can see how we fare and at the same time I can look for a place to set up home."

"I still don't think it's a good idea," Miles felt obliged to point out.

A maid knocked on the door, preventing Edith from replying to her brother. She was handed two letters by the servant. After she had left, Miles looked at Edith askew. "Anything I should be worrying about?"

"Pfft. You should work on these trust issues you have," she scolded. "Letters from Susan and Lady Pensby. Have you any objections to either of those?"

"No. Although I think keeping in touch with Lady Pensby will just keep your feelings to do with Pensby a little raw, do you not agree? Distance is usually better in these cases."

"Miles! Is there something you'd like to share with me? That sounds like the voice of experience," Edith said archly.

"Not at all. But I have eyes," Miles said with a shrug.

"Well my eyes are going to study these letters, so I shall leave you be," Edith said, standing and moving to the door. She paused before leaving. "You really do need to stop worrying about me. I'll be fine."

Entering the hallway, she blew out her cheeks. How she'd not given herself away in front of Miles, she had no idea. Recognising the handwriting on one of the letters had nearly sent her into a spasm. Ralph had written to her. The second letter she'd told the truth about, it was from Susan, but she could not have admitted the truth of the first letter to Miles.

Barely able to wait until she closed the door on her chamber, she tore at the seal and opened the letter.

Dear Miss S,

Please don't burn this letter, not until you have given me the chance to explain myself, although I realise I don't deserve your understanding.

What I've done is unforgivable. I know it now and I knew it from the start. Which I suppose makes my actions even worse, but I've promised myself I'll always be honest with you from now on. A decision I'm currently thinking I perhaps haven't thought through fully.

My actions don't excuse the matter that I needed to speak to someone and my first instinct was to turn to you. I suppose in another life, things would have been so different, but who knows? I was speaking the truth when I said you were my anchor. For the first time ever, I could say a little of what was troubling me. I admit to hoping that as you read my words there will be a stirring of the sympathy for which you are renowned by those who regard you. I hope for my sake, my gamble is paying off.

The expression on your face as we parted that last time, is haunting my nights. It is my last image of you and although I long to recount your smiling face, your laugh, your face as I kissed you, I can't shake off the look you gave me when I hurt you with my words. I am so sorry that I caused you such pain.

Since I've met you, it's as if you have crawled into my being and filled my every thought. Now I am bereft at your loss, even though it is as a result of my own actions.

If I thought it would help, I would beg an audience with you, to ask your forgiveness, but I dare not. To receive your refusal, would take away the one last grain of hope that I have to see you again.

I don't think I will ever be at peace if I am prevented from being in your company once more.

Are you cursing me to the devil? Are you laughing at my stupidity? Are you angry with my audacity? Do whatever makes you feel better, but I hope that a little part of your heart can go some way to forgiving me. In time perhaps.

Your servant,

Mr S

Edith put her head in her hands after reading the letter through three times in quick succession. Groaning, she scrunched the letter in her fist. "What are you trying to do to me? Torture me? Because it's working!" she whispered fiercely at the innate piece of paper.

Putting the letter into the drawer which had a lock to it, she turned to the letter from her friend. "I refuse to reply and give you any encouragement," she muttered to herself.

*

Two days later Edith received another letter. She was in the library, alone, and thankful that Miles was outside testing himself on horseback to see how his wounds stood up to the exercise.

Breaking the seal, her heart sped up. She hadn't replied and yet he'd written again.

My Dear Miss S,

I can only presume my words helped to keep you warm as they burned in your fire. It saddens me, but I can't say I blame you.

My mother is well and sends her love, which sort of takes the magic away from writing a love letter, when it is filled with regards from a parent.

Did I mention these were going to be love letters? I don't suppose I did. After our last set of correspondence I can understand if you are suspicious of the fact, but believe me when I say they are.

After you left, I came to realise that I'm not whole without you. The thought terrifies me, but it is the truth. I was taken to task by my darling mother – who is far too fond of you for my liking. If my wishes were to come true, I'm afraid I would never win an argument, with you both always sticking together.

That would be a small price to pay to have you by my side for the rest of my life. For that is what I want. Do I speak out of turn? Probably. At the moment I am prevented from seeing you, so this is my only form of communication.

I was mistaken you see. I thought that if I didn't marry or have children I could keep my mother safe and with me for as long as I possible. I just couldn't face the thought of losing her. It was only after your visit and talking to my mother that I realised I'd been mistaken. I can't control what happens to her. I can provide the best medical help we can find and all the comfort and support she needs when she's had one of her episodes, but I can't stop the reality of one day losing her. No matter what I do.

In truth, all I was doing was preventing myself from being happy and that was brought home to me when I met you. All of a sudden my future looked bleak, because you would not be in it. I have sat and wondered how many children we would have and if they would all be as beautiful as their mother, and then I would ache with longing to be with you. From first meeting you, I could never again be content with my foolish choices.

Edith, I've loved you from the first time we met. From the moment you walked down those stairs in Curzon Street, I was completely besotted.

Please find it in your heart to one day forgive my foolish behaviour.

Yours always,

Mr S

Edith rested her head against the sofa back on which she was seated. He'd all but proposed to her! The one thing she wanted more than anything and he'd done it.

Not knowing what to think or how to act, she read and reread the letter. There was no doubt, he was declaring his feelings for her. "You silly man," she quietly cursed. "How the devil am I going to respond to you?"

It was true, if she wrote back and asked Miles to frank her letter, he would either refuse outright, or immediately want to know exactly what was going on. Knowing Miles, he'd probably ride over to Lymewood and give Ralph the beating he'd promised him previously.

She could take the letter to the village and post it at the post office, but that would cause gossip and Miles would surely get to hear about it. She could send a letter to Lady Pensby, but somehow that felt wrong. There was also the chance that Lady Pensby would read Edith's words and her cheeks burned at even the thought of that.

No. She couldn't do anything, which meant Ralph wouldn't realise she'd been affected by his words and would probably give up.

She could have cursed as well as any man ever did.

Chapter 24

My Dear Miss S,

I have decided to take matters into my own hands. If you are ignoring my letters at least you haven't written to ask that I stop writing.

Bearing that in mind, I am going to become a man of action and for once in my life, fight for what I want.

I just hope you still want me.

Yours always

Mr S

Ralph was taking one heck of a risk. He could be met at the door by an army of staff, all led by an angry Miles. Or an angry Edith, come to that.

The days between sending the letters had been torture. He'd wanted her to reply, waiting every moment to be handed a letter, but although his ears had strained at every noise, no missive had been delivered.

"She won't trust you again so easily," Lady Pensby had soothed as her son paraded backwards and forwards across her bedchamber.

"I know. But even if she sent me a letter cursing me to the Americas and back, I would at least know how she feels and whether my efforts are wasted," Ralph said.

"You can't expect her to fall into your arms, metaphorically speaking of course. It was always going to be harder because she can't see that you are in earnest."

"That's it, isn't it? I'll have to go to her," Ralph said. "If she won't believe my words, I'll speak to her face-to-face."

"You will still need to tread carefully," Lady Pensby cautioned.

"I'll have to work out a way of actually seeing her first. Longdon is hardly likely to welcome me with open arms after the threat from his lips he left me with."

"You will have to control your temper. No fighting to rid yourself of all this frustration," Lady Pensby cautioned.

Ralph smiled. "I'm hardly likely to land a punch when I'm hoping to persuade him I'm the man for his sister."

"Good. Now go with my blessing and bring yourself back a wife."

"I wonder if she'll marry here?" Ralph asked.

Lady Pensby smiled. "I won't expect you to wait. Why not get yourself a special licence and have done with it?"

"Mother! Are you really suggesting we marry in such a way?" Ralph asked, aghast.

"Of course. I don't want you to have any opportunity for foolish thoughts to creep in on your part. Lady Edith is perfect for you. I knew that the moment I set eyes on her. Now, go and get yourself a bride and me a daughter," Lady Pensby instructed.

Ralph approached the bed and kissed his mother's head which was wrapped in a lace cap. "Fine. I'll do exactly as you wish, but when the house is full of a dozen brats, don't complain that there are too many children."

"Never, you foolish boy! God speed, my son."

*

Ralph had stayed in the next village to where the Longdon family lived. He didn't want any hint of his actual arrival to be passed to the house. His letter had given enough clues.

Having had a poor night's sleep, he rose early and set out for Barrowfoot House. He'd brought no valet with him, just a small bag and his horse. After making his decision, there'd been no point in delaying, so travelling on horseback was the quickest way of reaching Edith.

Riding sedately down the drive at Barrowfoot House, he was able to admire the parkland. It was in Hampshire, a county with rolling hills rather than mountains, but it had a pleasing aspect. It had taken him two hard days travel and he'd arrived late the previous night, causing a little suspicion of being some sort of ne'er do well when he'd first arrived at the inn.

Now, he was actually going to find out whether or not his journey had been in vain. The driveway opened up to reveal a limestone built Palladian house. It looked modern and impeccable and to the now slightly daunted Ralph, a little intimidating.

As he dismounted, the door was opened by a footman. "I'm here to see Lord Longdon," he said.

"He's away from home at the moment, sir."

"Is Lady Edith at home?" Ralph asked.

"If you'd like to step in, sir, I shall take your card."

Ralph stepped into the square marble hallway. Handing the footman his card, he was shown to a small anteroom with a side table and chairs. Unable to sit, Ralph paced the small room. At least Miles wasn't there. He didn't want to deceive his friend, but he also didn't want to see him quite yet, only the etiquette of his situation had caused him to ask for Miles first.

The footman returned and asked Ralph to follow him. Leading him to a ground floor drawing room, he opened the door for Ralph and stood back as he entered.

Edith had risen as Ralph walked through the doorway. She nodded dismissal to the footman and then turned her attention to Ralph. "Lord Pensby."

This wasn't a good start, Ralph thought as he looked at the impassive expression on Edith's face. "Lady Edith, forgive me, I could wait no longer. I had to see you," he said, taking a step towards her then faltering as his courage failed him a little.

Edith remained standing. "I see."

"Am I too late? Did I destroy your good opinion forever?" Ralph asked. "Tell me my case isn't completely hopeless."

"No."

"No? You have decided against me?"

"I haven't decided anything. For I don't fully know what is being offered," Edith admitted. She was watching closely, trying not to be affected by his pale face and worried expression. He looked younger and more vulnerable as he stared at her, seeming to be waiting for the slightest hint of her feelings.

Ralph placed his hat and gloves on the nearest couch. He'd kept hold of them whilst in the hallway, needing to grip onto something. Stepping closer to Edith, he held out his hands. "I offer you everything. My heart. My soul. My life. My love," he said quietly.

Calm, Edith thought. Taking a steadying breath, she was able to sound tolerably unmoved. "But you had such firm opinions on marriage that you were extremely keen to share. What could possibly have changed to alter that?"

"You changed me," Ralph admitted. "It was easy to ignore what I wanted whilst I hadn't met anyone who I would consider spending even a month with, let alone the rest of my life."

"But even with me, you made it quite clear you weren't looking for marriage," Edith pointed out.

"I was trying to push you away. I suppose without any conscious thought behind it. I presumed if I could reject you, my feelings would stop," Ralph answered. "It didn't work."

"I have to ask," Edith started. "Has this anything to do with your mother's wishes?"

"What? No. Although she does like you."

"If I thought for one moment that she'd persuaded you to offer for me because she wants to see you married, you can take yourself off—"

Ralph took two strides and stopping Edith from speaking in the best way that he could, he wrapped her in his arms and kissed her.

This wasn't the kiss they'd previously shared; this was a kiss of passion, of showing what words couldn't say. A kiss that expressed feelings he'd so long tried to ignore.

Edith had not hesitated in wrapping her hands around Ralph's neck and pulling him towards her. She'd wanted to be in his arms since he'd walked through the door, but had waited until she was sure of him. As he kissed her with such feeling, cupping her face in his hands then moving them to pull her body against his, she could no longer question his intent.

Eventually, Ralph rested his head against Edith's forehead. "I've wanted to kiss you like that since the moment I met you."

"Now, I'll have no flummery from you. You didn't wish that at all," Edith scolded gently, while twisting her fingers into his hair.

"I damn well did," Ralph said, nipping her lip gently. "How I managed to keep my hands off you until we shared that brief kiss, I'll never know. I have dreamed about seeing your eyes warm as they did then."

"And I'd like you to take your hands off my sister and tell me why it would seem that you've kissed her not once, but twice," came the rumbling voice of Miles.

Both Ralph and Edith jumped apart, but Ralph held his arm around Edith's waist in a protective gesture. "I asked to see you first, but was told you were out," he responded to Miles.

Closing the door behind him, Miles came further into the room. "So you decided to compromise my sister, even though you've no intention of marrying her."

"I've every intention of marrying her, if she'll have me," Ralph glanced at Edith, a shy smile lifting his lips.

"Edith, I would strongly advise against it," Miles said glaring at Ralph. "You were right what you said when we visited him – he's no different to Sage. He took advantage of the information I'd given him to get close to you, but then, even worse than that rake, he rejected you. Are you really going to forgive him for that?"

Edith flushed. "I-I'm confused." She felt Ralph moving away from her and looked at him in alarm.

"I'm not going to force you into anything you don't want to do," he said gently. "My feelings won't change. I promise you that, but I want you to come to me not because you've been persuaded by me or your situation, but because you want me above all others."

"You know I loved you, don't you?" Edith asked, cheeks aflame.

"Yes. When you thought I'd betrayed you, you mentioned the fact," Ralph said. "I hope one day that you'll come to love me again, for it seems I managed to turn your feelings against me, like the buffoon I am."

"I'm sorry. I was overcome with seeing you and acted like some sort of hoyden," Edith said. "I'd like a little time to think."

"Of course," Ralph said, trying to hide the crushing defeat he felt. "I shall leave you, but I will be staying at the Cheshire Oak inn a few miles away. Do you know it?"

Edith nodded.

"Good. Send me a message and I will return immediately. If I haven't heard from you in three days, I'll presume you can't forgive my past folly and I'll return home," Ralph said.

He turned and picked up his hat and gloves from where he'd discarded them and nodded to Miles. He paused at the glower he received. "Don't blame your sister for what's happened here today and in the past. I've chased her and want to worship her for the rest of my days. I know you wish me to the devil, but I didn't purposely set out to deceive you and if she says yes, your disapproval won't stand in our way. I would like your blessing, but I don't need it."

"Get out," Miles growled, his fists clenching at his side.

Chapter 25

"Why? Why after all he's done to hurt you would you be wrapped around him like you were? Have you no self-respect?" Miles hissed once Ralph had gone.

"Of course I have!" Edith retorted, her face aflame. "Why have you suddenly set yourself so much against him? What do you know that would make you dislike him so much?"

Miles walked deeper into the room and poured himself a large measure of brandy. "I don't know anything," he said before taking a large gulp of the liquid.

"Then I don't understand your objection," Edith shrugged.

"He's hurt you and used you. You said so yourself. Why would you forgive him? How could you trust him after that?"

"Miles, who has hurt you so much that you'd react so harshly?" Edith asked gently.

"No one! I'm just looking out for my sister. Is that so wrong?" Miles asked.

"No. And I appreciate it but only up to a point. You have to understand something about your friend," Edith started.

"He's no blasted friend of mine anymore."

"Now you sound like a child!" Edith exclaimed. "You're better than that. Lord Pensby has been mistaken in his outlook of life because of his mother's illness. He was living his life in the way he thought was best for both of them, but recently, things have changed for him."

"How?"

"He met me and apparently I set the cat amongst the birds," Edith smiled.

"And he's told you this?"

"Yes, you suspicious creature, but his mother also hinted that she thought he had feelings for me, long before anyone knew of the letters. In fact, they'd stopped at that point by his instigation actually," Edith said.

Miles grunted.

"I've had plenty of time to think over his actions," Edith said.

"And you were affected so little by them that you've been trying to throw yourself over every tricky fence and hedge within a ten-mile radius," Miles said sarcastically.

"That stopped over a week ago," Edith responded.

"When you injured your horse," Miles pointed out.

"When I received a letter from him."

Edith chose not to respond to the curse which Miles uttered at her words.

"I've been thinking of little else and no, before you ask, I didn't respond to his communication. If you like it was a sort of test for him by me," Edith admitted.

"How so?"

"I wanted to see how he would respond to a rebuke. It wasn't a written one, admittedly, but I couldn't reply to his correspondence without you finding out and I wanted to make my decisions without your input. Sorry."

"You are too independent sometimes."

"I've had to be," Edith said matter-of-fact.

"I know."

"Which is why it was important to come to my own conclusions."

"From the way you were embracing him at my entrance, I presume you had already done so?"

"Yes," Edith smiled.

"Then why the hesitation when I arrived?"

"I wanted to speak to you. This hatred of Lord Pensby can't continue if I am to marry him. It isn't like you, Miles. You are one of the most easy-going people I know," Edith said.

"I used to be perhaps," Miles admitted. He sighed. "You're right. Life is too short to get caught up in silly feuds. I'll be on my best behaviour the next time I see Pensby."

Edith crossed to her brother and sat beside him. "Thank you, Miles. You are the second most important person in the world to me. It really means something to know you are happy for me."

"I don't need to ask who the first one is. I'll be happy when I see him treating you well and loving you as you should be," Miles admitted grudgingly.

"Oh, he will. I'm sure of it."

"There is another person who'll be ecstatic about the match," Miles pointed out with a flicker of a smile.

"Mother!" Edith groaned. "She's going to be a nightmare with wedding preparations. It could be enough to put me off the whole thing."

"Don't make jokes like that at the moment. Let me become accustomed to liking Pensby again, before you make flippant quips."

"Sorry," Edith smiled. "But before we tell Mother, I'd best arrange to visit my betrothed, or soon to be at least."

"Send him a letter and ask him to call," Miles said.

"No. I think what I have to say needs to be said on neutral ground. I'll arrange for the carriage to be brought around."

"You could always wait until tomorrow?" Miles suggested.

"I didn't know you had such a cruel streak in you! Fancy leaving the poor man to suffer overnight," Edith chided.

"It'll do him the world of good."

"Miles!"

"I'll send for the carriage."

*

The more the wheels turned as the vehicle moved along the roads, the more Edith became jittery. Trying to work out what she would say only made her worse, so instead, she sat, chewing the bottom of her lip as she was driven to the Cheshire Oak.

The inn was bustling when she arrived, but a footman was soon directed to find out if Ralph was in and if he had a private parlour. Within a few minutes she was led by the innkeeper and followed by the footman, to the downstairs parlour.

Ralph jumped up, his face looking equally full of hope and doubt. The innkeeper retreated, but the footman looked to remain with Edith.

"That will be all," Edith instructed. "You can wait with the carriage. If I need you I shall send word."

"But his Lordship..." the loyal servant started.

"Can be a trifle demanding, I know," Edith said. "Don't worry. There won't be any repercussions for you."

"Yes, m'lady," came the meek response, and the door was closed as the servant left.

"Your brother will curse me to the devil when he knows you've allowed yourself to be in here unprotected," Ralph said.

"We did exactly the same when the same foolish brother decided to fight with a highwayman and I came to no harm then, I'm sure I'll be fine," Edith said, removing her bonnet and gloves and acting far calmer than she felt.

"I suppose so," Ralph acknowledged. "Am I to hope you bring good news?"

"Miles isn't going to kill you, if that's what you mean," Edith said.

Ralph's lips twitched. "You aren't going to make this easy, are you?"

"No."

"I thought seeing you so soon was too good to be true."

"I'd like to ask you some questions first, if you've no objections?" Edith said, but her voice contained a laugh.

"Of course. Please be seated."

"I'd rather stand."

"As you wish."

"What state are your finances in?" Edith asked.

"I am increasing my family's wealth, not decreasing it," Ralph blinked in response.

"I suppose that's through the gambling winnings you take," Edith said airily. "At least it seems you can't be accused of being a fortune hunter."

"No."

"Do you want children?"

"Yes. Lots, especially if they are like their mother."

Edith swallowed. "Will you insist on going to London for the season every year?"

"No. The love of my life would prefer to rusticate and so would I."

"What about embarrassing relatives?"

"My mother is an acquired taste, but she does improve on getting to know her."

Edith laughed. "You brute! You knew full well I was referring to my own mother."

"I was being serious, you haven't spent long enough in my mother's company to know her faults."

"Mine will probably want to visit."

Ralph took a step towards Edith. When she didn't move away from him, he took another and another until he was standing directly in front of her. "If I have you as my wife, nothing else will matter. Not relatives who frustrate us, people who talk about us, none of it will affect me because I'll have you."

"You really should write poetry, you have a way with words."

"I tried writing letters, but there was too much which could go wrong. I'm going to rely on the spoken word in future," Ralph said. "Do we have a future, Edith?"

"My mother will be appalling whilst we plan the wedding. Are you sure you want to do this? I can promise you, your patience will be tested," Edith said, needing to point out all the issues he was going to be faced with.

"Ah, I have something for you," Ralph said, pulling the paper out of his pocket. "If you ever say yes to my proposal, which I have to point out that you haven't done so yet. But if you do, then there is this which might help solve all our problems."

Edith took the paper and after reading it, looked at Ralph in surprise. "A special licence?"

Wrapping his arms around Edith and drawing her to him, he kissed her nose. "If you want a large, fancy wedding planned by your mother, that's what we'll have. I say that most willingly. If you ask me what I want, that would be to marry you as soon as we can find a minister. Then we can send an express to your mother, telling her the deed is done, place a notice in *The Times*, and then I'll take you home."

"*The Times*? In the Advertisement Section?" Edith asked.

"Of course. Where else? But it's your choice. No pressure for either way. I'll still get to have you as my wife. That's all I really want."

"The special licence is perfect, as long as Miles will be there," Edith said, smiling.

"Of course. You do need him to walk you down the aisle after all. Is that a yes, then?"

"I suppose it is," Edith shrugged, which turned into a laugh as she was swung off her feet and spun around.

"Thank goodness for that!" Ralph said, finally placing her on the floor. "I'd run out of ideas of what to do next if you refused me. All I'd come up with was taking on a farm on your estate and becoming a farmer who followed you around every day."

"As much as I'd like that, I'd prefer to have you by my side as my husband," Edith said. All other words were lost as Ralph kissed her without restraint.

*

My darling Miss S,

This is our wedding day and although it has been moments since we were together, it already feels too long.

I will thank the gods, my stars, and a four-leaf clover I once found, for being able to have you beside me as we vow to spend the rest of our lives together.

You have not only made me the happiest of men, but I now can look forward to a bright future, instead of the dark, lonely one I had anticipated. To say you have changed my life is an understatement. Thank you, my darling.

Every day I promise to prove to you how much you mean to me, how beautiful I think you are, how much you make me laugh. I never want to make you unhappy but I'm sure there will be times when you will curse me. Know this though, I shall never, even in our darkest moments, ever stop loving you.

Yours always and with a heart full of love
Mr S

Edith dabbed her eyes and tucked the letter in her reticule. It would be added to the others later, but she didn't have time to put it in a safe place at the moment.

Miles came around the corner of the church. "You look very pretty, Edith. He's a lucky man," he said in a choked voice. "Are you ready?"

Edith smiled at her brother. Kissing his cheek, she placed her hand on his arm. "I'm ready," she said as they walked through the door to the chapel.

Epilogue

Notice in *The Times* Advertisement Section:-
Lady Edith Longdon (Miss S) married Lord Pensby (Mr S) on the third day of the month in a quiet ceremony near the bride's home. Brought together by this column, they have kindly given permission that their names be revealed to encourage all the other lonely hearts' readers, that you will one day also find your fellow lonely heart. This newspaper wishes them all the very best for their future happiness.

Ralph wrote letters to Edith regularly throughout their marriage. She treasured each and every one. They were to have six lively, healthy children, who filled Lymewood with enough noise to make up for lost time. Ralph very often was the one suggesting the noisiest games.

Lady Pensby moved into the Dower House without incident and became a very precious granny. Lady Longdon chose to set up home in London and rarely travelled to see her daughter and son-in-law, although she spoke about them often.

Miles forgot his antagonism towards Ralph very soon after the marriage when the evidence of his sister's happiness was plain to see by everyone coming into contact with the pair. He eventually would spend a lot of time with the couple, but in the first instance – well, he had his own story to finish...

Miss King's Rescue.

The second part of the Lonely Hearts' Series

Available April 2020!

About this book.

I love the films *You've Got Mail* and *The Shop Around the Corner*. They are funny, sweet and lovely movies. I think they portray how much can be conveyed via letters and how we can connect to people in a different way to face-to-face interactions. I love getting newsy emails and letters.

I then discovered Lonely Hearts' Columns go back as far as the 1600s and were very popular. When I found that out, it was inevitable that a story about an advertisement and writing letters would appear at some point!

It was going to be a standalone story, but very often as I write, characters develop who need their own story and that's what happened with Miles and Susan. They're now going to have their own adventure.

With regards to the epilepsy Lady Pensby suffered from, it was a condition which was linked to being possessed by a devil, or as a form of punishment by the gods for hundreds of years. By the Georgian era, it was at last recognised as an illness. You won't be surprised to know the solutions were pretty grim and mostly unsuccessful. The drug I mentioned being used by Napoleon's troops was actually hashish and was banned by Napoleon because it made his troops less able to fight! Cannabis was used historically as an herbal remedy for epilepsy, so I thought I could pinch Napoleon's soldiers' discovery to help Lady Pensby. Chinese herbs were also used, but it was only in the Victorian period that major advances started to occur.

I hope you enjoyed Edith and Ralph's journey as much as I enjoyed writing and researching it! If you could leave a review, I'd be really grateful – they help enormously to independent authors. Thanks as always for your support.
Audrey

About the Author

I have had the fortune to live a dream. I've always wanted to write, but life got in the way as it so often does until a few years ago. Then a change in circumstance enabled me to do what I loved: sit down to write. Now writing has taken over my life, holidays being based around research, so much so that no matter where we go, my long-suffering husband says, 'And what connection to the Regency period has this building/town/garden got?'

That dream became a little more surreal when in 2018, I became an Amazon StorytellerUK Finalist with Lord Livesey's Bluestocking. A Regency Romance in the top five of an all-genre competition! It was a truly wonderful experience, I didn't expect to win, but I had a ball at the awards ceremony.

I do appreciate it when readers get in touch, especially if they love the characters as much as I do. Those first few weeks after release is a trying time; I desperately want everyone to love my characters that take months and months of work to bring to life.

If you enjoy the books please would you take the time to write a review on Amazon? Reviews are vital for an author who is just starting out, although I admit to bad ones being crushing. Selfishly I want readers to love my stories!

I can be contacted for any comments you may have, via my website:

www.audreyharrison.co.uk
or
www.facebook.com/AudreyHarrisonAuthor

Please sign-up for email/newsletter – only sent out when there is something to say!

www.audreyharrison.co.uk

You'll receive a free copy of The Unwilling Earl in mobi format for signing-up as a thank you!

Novels by Audrey Harrison

Regency Romances – newest release first

The Lonely Lord
https://www.amazon.com/dp/B07S1X5NBZ
https://www.amazon.co.uk/dp/B07S1X5NBZ
The Drummond Series:-
Lady Lou the Highwayman – Drummond series Book 1
https://www.amazon.com/dp/B07NDX3HV2
https://www.amazon.co.uk/dp/B07NDX3HV2
Saving Captain Drummond – Drummond Series Book 2
https://www.amazon.com/dp/B07NFBRZFG
https://www.amazon.co.uk/dp/B07NFBRZFG

Lord Livesey's Bluestocking (Amazon Storyteller Finalist 2018)
https://www.amazon.com/dp/B07D3T6L93
https://www.amazon.co.uk/dp/B07D3T6L93
Return to the Regency – A Regency Time-travel novel
https://www.amazon.com/dp/B078C87HVX
https://www.amazon.co.uk/dp/B078C87HVX
My Foundlings:-
The Foundling Duke – The Foundlings Book 1

https://www.amazon.com/dp/B071KTT9CD
https://www.amazon.co.uk/dp/B071KTT9CD
The Foundling Lady – The Foundlings Book 2
https://www.amazon.com/dp/B072L2D7PF
https://www.amazon.co.uk/dp/B072L2D7PF
Book bundle – **The Foundlings**
https://www.amazon.com/dp/B07Q6YLND4
https://www.amazon.co.uk/dp/B07Q6YLND4
Mr Bailey's Lady
https://www.amazon.com/dp/B01NACMFVJ
https://www.amazon.co.uk/dp/B01NACMFVJ
The Spy Series:-
My Lord the Spy
https://www.amazon.com/dp/B01F11ZRM8
https://www.amazon.co.uk/dp/B01F11ZRM8
My Earl the Spy
https://www.amazon.com/dp/B01F12NG8E
https://www.amazon.co.uk/dp/B01F12NG8E
Book bundle – **The Spying Lords**
https://www.amazon.com/dp/B07RV3JQFP
https://www.amazon.co.uk/dp/B07RV3JQFP
The Captain's Wallflower
https://www.amazon.com/dp/B018PDBGLK
https://www.amazon.co.uk/dp/B018PDBGLK
The Four Sisters' Series:-
Rosalind – Book 1
https://www.amazon.com/dp/B00WWTXSA6
https://www.amazon.co.uk/dp/B00WWTXSA6
Annabelle – Book 2
https://www.amazon.com/dp/B00WWTXRWA
https://www.amazon.co.uk/dp/B00WWTXRWA
Grace – Book 3
https://www.amazon.com/dp/B00WWUBEWO

https://www.amazon.co.uk/dp/B00WWUBEWO
Eleanor – Book 4
https://www.amazon.com/dp/B00WWUBF1E
https://www.amazon.co.uk/dp/B00WWUBF1E
Book Bundle – **The Four Sisters**
https://www.amazon.com/dp/B01416W0C4
https://www.amazon.co.uk/dp/B01416W0C4
The Inconvenient Trilogy:-
The Inconvenient Ward – Book 1
https://www.amazon.com/dp/B00KCJUJFA
https://www.amazon.co.uk/dp/B00KCJUJFA
The Inconvenient Wife – Book 2
https://www.amazon.com/dp/B00KCJVQU2
https://www.amazon.co.uk/dp/B00KCJVQU2
The Inconvenient Companion – Book 3
https://www.amazon.com/dp/B00KCK87T4
https://www.amazon.co.uk/dp/B00KCK87T4
Book bundle – **An Inconvenient Trilogy**
https://www.amazon.com/dp/B00PHQIZ18
https://www.amazon.co.uk/dp/B00PHQIZ18
The Complicated Earl
https://www.amazon.com/dp/B00BCN90DC
https://www.amazon.co.uk/dp/B00BCN90DC
The Unwilling Earl (Novella)
https://www.amazon.com/dp/B00BCNE2HG
https://www.amazon.co.uk/dp/B00BCNE2HG

Other Eras
A Very Modern Lord
Years Apart

Printed in Great Britain
by Amazon